THE UNCOMMON READER

Alan Bennett has been one of our leading dramatists since the success of *Beyond the Fringe* in the 1960s. His television series *Talking Heads* has become a modern-day classic, as have many of his works for the stage, including *Forty Years On*, *The Lady in the Van*, *A Question of Attribution*, *The Madness of George III* (together with the Oscar-nominated screenplay *The Madness of King George*), and an adaptation of Kenneth Grahame's *The Wind in the Willows*. At the National Theatre, London, *The History Boys* won numerous awards including Evening Standard and Critics' Circle awards for Best Play, an Olivier for Best New Play and the South Bank Award. On Broadway, *The History Boys* won five New York Drama Desk Awards, four Outer Critics' Circle Awards, a New York Drama Critics' Award and six Tonys. *The Habit of Art* opened at the National in 2009; in 2012, *People*, as well as the two short plays *Hymn* and *Cocktail Sticks*, was also staged there. His collection of prose *Writing Home* was a number one bestseller. *Untold Stories* won the PEN/Ackerley Prize for autobiography, 2006. Recent works are *The Uncommon Reader*, *Smut: Two Unseemly Stories*, *Keeping On Keeping On* and *Two Besides: A Pair of Talking Heads*.

The Uncommon Reader

ALAN BENNETT

faber

P

PROFILE BOOKS

First published in 2006 in the *London Review of Books*
28 Little Russell Street, London WC1A 2HN

First published in hardback in 2007
by Faber and Faber Ltd
74–77 Great Russell Street
London WC1B 3DA

and

Profile Books Ltd
29 Cloth Fair
London EC1A 7JQ

This paperback edition first published in 2008, reprinted in 2021

Typeset by Faber and Faber Ltd
Printed in England by CPI Group (UK) Ltd, Croydon CR0 4YY

A CIP record for this book
is available from the British Library

ISBN 978 1 78816 806 9
eISBN 978 1 84765 338 3

THE UNCOMMON READER

AT WINDSOR it was the evening of the state banquet and as the president of France took his place beside Her Majesty, the royal family formed up behind and the procession slowly moved off and through into the Waterloo Chamber.

'Now that I have you to myself,' said the Queen, smiling to left and right as they glided through the glittering throng, 'I've been longing to ask you about the writer Jean Genet.'

'Ah,' said the president. 'Oui.'

The 'Marseillaise' and the national anthem made for a pause in the proceedings, but when they had taken their seats Her Majesty turned to the president and resumed.

'Homosexual and jailbird, was he nevertheless as bad as he was painted? Or, more to the point' – and she took up her soup spoon – 'was he as good?'

Unbriefed on the subject of the glabrous play-wright and novelist, the president looked wildly about for his minister of culture. But she was being addressed by the Archbishop of Canterbury.

'Jean Genet,' said the Queen again, helpfully. 'Vous le connaissez?'

'Bien sûr,' said the president.

'Il m'intéresse,' said the Queen.

'Vraiment?' The president put down his spoon. It was going to be a long evening.

IT WAS the dogs' fault. They were snobs and ordinar-ily, having been in the garden, would have gone up the front steps, where a footman generally opened them the door. Today, though, for some reason they careered along the terrace, barking their heads off, and scampered down the steps again and round the end along the side of the house, where she could hear them yapping at something in one of the yards.

It was the City of Westminster travelling library, a large removal-like van parked next to the bins out-side one of the kitchen doors. This wasn't a part of the palace she saw much of, and she had certainly

{ 4 }

never seen the library there before, nor presumably had the dogs, hence the din, so having failed in her attempt to calm them down she went up the little steps of the van in order to apologise.

The driver was sitting with his back to her, sticking a label on a book, the only seeming borrower a thin ginger-haired boy in white overalls crouched in the aisle reading. Neither of them took any notice of the new arrival, so she coughed and said, 'I'm sorry about this awful racket,' whereupon the driver got up so suddenly he banged his head on the Reference section and the boy in the aisle scrambled to his feet and upset Photography & Fashion.

She put her head out of the door. 'Shut up this minute, you silly creatures' – which, as had been the move's intention, gave the driver/librarian time to compose himself and the boy to pick up the books.

'One has never seen you here before, Mr . . .'

'Hutchings, Your Majesty. Every Wednesday, ma'am.'

'Really? I never knew that. Have you come far?'

'Only from Westminster, ma'am.'

'And you are . . . ?'

'Norman, ma'am. Seakins.'

'And where do you work?'

'In the kitchen, ma'am.'

'Oh. Do you have much time for reading?'

'Not really, ma'am.'

'I'm the same. Though now that one is here I suppose one ought to borrow a book.'

Mr Hutchings smiled helpfully.

'Is there anything you would recommend?'

'What does Your Majesty like?'

The Queen hesitated, because to tell the truth she wasn't sure. She'd never taken much interest in reading. She read, of course, as one did, but liking books was something she left to other people. It was a hobby and it was in the nature of her job that she didn't have hobbies. Jogging, growing roses, chess or rock-climbing, cake decoration, model aeroplanes. No. Hobbies involved preferences and preferences had to be avoided; preferences excluded people. One had no preferences. Her job was to take an interest, not to be interested herself. And besides, reading wasn't doing. She was a doer. So she gazed round the book-lined van and played for time. 'Is one allowed to borrow a book? One doesn't have a ticket?'

'No problem,' said Mr Hutchings.

'One is a pensioner,' said the Queen, not that she was sure that made any difference.

'Ma'am can borrow up to six books.'

'Six? Heavens!'

Meanwhile the ginger-haired young man had made his choice and given his book to the librarian to stamp. Still playing for time, the Queen picked it up.

'What have you chosen, Mr Seakins?' expecting it to be, well, she wasn't sure what she expected, but it wasn't what it was. 'Oh. Cecil Beaton. Did you know him?'

'No, ma'am.'

'No, of course not. You'd be too young. He always used to be round here, snapping away. And a bit of a tartar. Stand here, stand there. Snap, snap. So there's a book about him now?'

'Several, ma'am.'

'Really? I suppose everyone gets written about sooner or later.'

She riffled through it. 'There's probably a picture of me in it somewhere. Oh yes. That one. Of course, he wasn't just a photographer. He designed, too. *Oklahoma*, things like that.'

'I think it was *My Fair Lady*, ma'am.'

'Oh, was it?' said the Queen, unused to being contradicted.

'Where did you say you worked?' She put the book back in the boy's big red hands.

'In the kitchens, ma'am.'

She had still not solved her problem, knowing that if she left without a book it would seem to Mr Hutchings that the library was somehow lacking. Then on a shelf of rather worn-looking volumes she saw a name she remembered. 'Ivy Compton-Burnett! I can read that.' She took the book out and gave it to Mr Hutchings to stamp.

'What a treat!' She hugged it unconvincingly before opening it. 'Oh. The last time it was taken out was in 1989.'

'She's not a popular author, ma'am.'

'Why, I wonder? I made her a dame.'

Mr Hutchings refrained from saying that this wasn't necessarily the road to the public's heart.

The Queen looked at the photograph on the back of the jacket. 'Yes. I remember that hair, a roll like a pie-crust that went right round her head.' She smiled and Mr Hutchings knew that the visit was over. 'Goodbye.'

He inclined his head as they had told him at the library to do should this eventuality ever arise, and the Queen went off in the direction of the garden with the dogs madly barking again, while Norman, bearing his Cecil Beaton, skirted a chef lounging by the bins having a cigarette and went back to the kitchens.

Shutting up the van and driving away, Mr Hutchings reflected that a novel by Ivy Compton-Burnett would take some reading. He had never got very far with her himself and thought, rightly, that borrowing the book had just been a polite gesture. Still, it was one that he appreciated and as more than a courtesy. The council was always threatening to cut back on the library and the patronage of so distinguished a borrower (or customer as the council preferred to call it) would do him no harm.

'We have a travelling library,' the Queen said to her husband that evening. 'Comes every Wednesday.'

'Jolly good. Wonders never cease.'

'You remember *Oklahoma*?'

'Yes. We saw it when we were engaged.' Extraordinary to think of it, the dashing blond boy he had been.

'Was that Cecil Beaton?' said the Queen.

'No idea. Never liked the fellow. Green shoes.'

'Smelled delicious.'

'What's that?'

'A book. I borrowed it.'

'Dead, I suppose.'

'Who?'

'The Beaton fellow.'

'Oh yes. Everybody's dead.'

'Good show, though.'

And he went off to bed glumly singing 'Oh, what a beautiful morning' as the Queen opened her book.

THE FOLLOWING week she had intended to give the book to a lady-in-waiting to return, but finding herself taken captive by her private secretary and forced to go through the diary in far greater detail than she thought necessary, she was able to cut off discussion of a tour round a road-research laboratory by suddenly declaring that it was Wednesday and she had to go to change her book at the travelling library. Her private secretary, Sir Kevin Scatchard, an over-conscientious New Zealander of whom great things were expected, was left to gather up his papers and wonder why ma'am needed a travelling library when she had several of the stationary kind of her own.

Minus the dogs this visit was somewhat calmer, though once again Norman was the only borrower.

'How did you find it, ma'am?' asked Mr Hutchings.

'Dame Ivy? A little dry. And everybody talks the same way, did you notice that?'

'To tell you the truth, ma'am, I never got through more than a few pages. How far did Your Majesty get?'

'Oh, to the end. Once I start a book I finish it. That was the way one was brought up. Books, bread and butter, mashed potato – one finishes what's on one's plate. That's always been my philosophy.'

'There was actually no need to have brought the book back, ma'am. We're downsizing and all the books on that shelf are free.'

'You mean, I can have it?' She clutched the book to her. 'I'm glad I came. Good afternoon, Mr Seakins. More Cecil Beaton?'

Norman showed her the book he was looking at,

this time something on David Hockney. She leafed through it, gazing unperturbed at young men's bottoms hauled out of Californian swimming-pools or lying together on unmade beds.

'Some of them,' she said, 'some of them don't seem altogether finished. This one is quite definitely smudged.'

'I think that was his style then, ma'am,' said Norman. 'He's actually quite a good draughtsman.'

The Queen looked at Norman again. 'You work in the kitchens?'

'Yes, ma'am.'

She hadn't really intended to take out another book, but decided that now she was here it was perhaps easier to do it than not, though, regarding what book to choose, she felt as baffled as she had done the previous week. The truth was she didn't really want a book at all and certainly not another Ivy Compton-Burnett, which was too hard going altogether. So it was lucky that this time her eye happened to fall on a reissued volume of Nancy Mitford's *The Pursuit of Love*. She picked it up. 'Now. Didn't her sister marry the Mosley man?'

Mr Hutchings said he believed she did.

'And the mother-in-law of another sister was my mistress of the robes?'

'I don't know about that, ma'am.'

'Then of course there was the rather sad sister who had the fling with Hitler. And one became a Communist. And I think there was another besides. But this is Nancy?'

'Yes, ma'am.'

'Good.'

Novels seldom came as well connected as this and the Queen felt correspondingly reassured, so it was with some confidence that she gave the book to Mr Hutchings to be stamped.

The Pursuit of Love turned out to be a fortunate choice and in its way a momentous one. Had Her Majesty gone for another duff read, an early George Eliot, say, or a late Henry James, novice reader that she was she might have been put off reading for good and there would be no story to tell. Books, she would have thought, were work.

As it was, with this one she soon became engrossed and, passing her bedroom that night clutching his hot-water bottle, the duke heard her laugh out loud. He put his head round the door. 'All right, old girl?'

'Of course. I'm reading.'

'Again?' And he went off, shaking his head.

The next morning she had a little sniffle and, having no engagements, stayed in bed saying she felt she might be getting flu. This was uncharacteristic and also not true; it was actually so that she could get on with her book.

'The Queen has a slight cold' was what the nation was told, but what it was not told, and what the Queen herself did not know, was that this was only the first of a series of accommodations, some of them far-reaching, that her reading was going to involve.

The following day the Queen had one of her regular sessions with her private secretary, with as one of the items on the agenda what these days is called human resources.

'In my day,' she had told him, 'it was called personnel.' Although actually it wasn't. It was called 'the servants'. She mentioned this, too, knowing it would provoke a reaction.

'That could be misconstrued, ma'am,' said Sir Kevin. 'One's aim is always to give the public no cause for offence. "Servants" sends the wrong message.'

'Human resources', said the Queen, 'sends no message at all. At least not to me. However, since we're on the subject of human resources, there is one human resource currently working in the kitchens whom I would like promoted, or at any rate brought upstairs.'

Sir Kevin had never heard of Seakins but on consulting several underlings Norman was eventually located.

'I cannot understand', said Her Majesty, 'what he is doing in the kitchen in the first place. He's obviously a young man of some intelligence.'

'Not dolly enough,' said the equerry, though to the private secretary not to the Queen. 'Thin, ginger-haired. Have a heart.'

'Madam seems to like him,' said Sir Kevin. 'She wants him on her floor.'

Thus it was that Norman found himself emancipated from washing dishes and fitted (with some difficulty) into a page's uniform and brought into waiting, where one of his first jobs was predictably to do with the library.

Not free the following Wednesday (gymnastics in Nuneaton), the Queen gave Norman her Nancy

Mitford to return, telling him that there was apparently a sequel and she wanted to read that too, plus anything else besides he thought she might fancy.

This commission caused him some anxiety. Well read up to a point, he was largely self-taught, his reading tending to be determined by whether an author was gay or not. Fairly wide remit though this was, it did narrow things down a bit, particularly when choosing a book for someone else, and the more so when that someone else happened to be the Queen.

Nor was Mr Hutchings much help, except that when he mentioned dogs as a subject that might interest Her Majesty it reminded Norman of something he had read that could fit the bill, J. R. Ackerley's novel *My Dog Tulip*. Mr Hutchings was dubious, pointing out that it was a gay book.

'Is it?' said Norman innocently. 'I didn't realise that. She'll think it's just about the dog.'

He took the books up to the Queen's floor and, having been told to make himself as scarce as possible, when the duke came by hid behind a boulle cabinet.

'Saw this extraordinary creature this afternoon,' HRH reported later. 'Ginger-stick-in-waiting.'

'That would be Norman,' said the Queen. 'I met him in the travelling library. He used to work in the kitchen.'

'I can see why,' said the duke.

'He's very intelligent,' said the Queen.

'He'll have to be,' said the duke. 'Looking like that.'

'Tulip,' said the Queen to Norman later. 'Funny name for a dog.'

'It's supposed to be fiction, ma'am, only the author did have a dog in life, an Alsatian.' (He didn't tell her its name was Queenie.) 'So it's really disguised autobiography.'

'Oh,' said the Queen. 'Why disguise it?'

Norman thought she would find out when she read the book, but he didn't say so.

'None of his friends liked the dog, ma'am.'

'One knows that feeling very well,' said the Queen, and Norman nodded solemnly, the royal dogs being generally unpopular. The Queen smiled. What a find Norman was. She knew that she inhibited, made people shy, and few of the servants behaved like themselves. Oddity though he was, Norman was himself and seemed incapable of being anything else. That was very rare.

The Queen, though, might have been less pleased had she known that Norman was unaffected by her because she seemed to him so ancient, her royalty obliterated by her seniority. Queen she might be but she was also an old lady, and since Norman's introduction to the world of work had been via an old people's home on Tyneside old ladies held no terrors for him. To Norman she was his employer, but her age made her as much patient as Queen and in both capacities to be humoured, though this was, it's true, before he woke up to how sharp she was and how much wasted.

She was also intensely conventional and when she had started to read she thought perhaps she ought to do some of it at least in the place set aside for the purpose, namely the palace library. But though it was called the library and was indeed lined with books, a book was seldom if ever read there. Ultimatums were delivered here, lines drawn, prayer books compiled and marriages decided upon, but should one want to curl up with a book the library was not the place. It was not easy even to lay hands on something to read, as on the open shelves, so called, the books were sequestered behind locked and gilded grilles. Many of them were priceless, which was another discouragement. No, if reading was to be done it were better done in a place not set aside for it. The Queen thought that there might be a lesson there and she went back upstairs.

Having finished the Nancy Mitford sequel, *Love in a Cold Climate*, the Queen was delighted to see she had written others, and though some of them seemed to be history she put them on her (newly started) reading list, which she kept in her desk. Meanwhile she got on with Norman's choice, *My Dog Tulip* by J. R. Ackerley. (Had she met him? She thought not.) She enjoyed the book if only because, as Norman had said, the dog in question seemed even more of a handful than hers and just about as unpopular. Seeing that Ackerley had written an autobiography, she sent Norman down to the London Library to borrow it. Patron of the London Library, she had seldom set foot in it and neither, of course, had Norman, but he came back full of wonder and excitement at how old-fashioned it was, saying it was the sort of library he had only read about in books and had thought confined to the past. He had wandered through its labyrinthine stacks marvelling that these were all books that he (or rather She) could borrow at will. So infectious was his enthusiasm that next time, the Queen thought, she might accompany him.

She read Ackerley's account of himself, unsurprised to find that, being a homosexual, he had worked for the BBC, though feeling also that he had had a sad life. His dog intrigued her, though she was disconcerted by the almost veterinary intimacies with which he indulged the creature. She was also surprised that the Guards seemed to be as readily available as the book made out and at such a reasonable tariff. She would have liked to have known more about this; but though she had equerries who were in the Guards she hardly felt able to ask.

E. M. Forster figured in the book, with whom she remembered spending an awkward half-hour when she invested him with the CH. Mouse-like and shy, he had said little and in such a small voice she had found him almost impossible to communicate with. Still, he was a bit of a dark horse. Sitting there with his hands pressed together like something out of *Alice in Wonderland*, he gave no hint of what he was thinking, and so she was pleasantly surprised to find on reading his biography that he had said afterwards that had she been a boy he would have fallen in love with her.

Of course he couldn't actually have said this to her face, she realised that, but the more she read the more she regretted how she intimidated people and wished that writers in particular had the courage to say what they later wrote down. What she was finding also was how one book led to another, doors kept opening wherever she turned and the days weren't long enough for the reading she wanted to do.

But there was regret, too, and mortification at the many opportunities she had missed. As a child she had met Masefield and Walter de la Mare; nothing much she could have said to them, but she had met T. S. Eliot, too, and there was Priestley and Philip Larkin and even Ted Hughes, to whom she'd taken a bit of a shine but who remained nonplussed in her presence. And it was because she had at that time read so little of what they had written that she could not find anything to say and they, of course, had not said much of interest to her. What a waste.

She made the mistake of mentioning this to Sir Kevin.

'But ma'am must have been briefed, surely?'

'Of course,' said the Queen, 'but briefing is not reading. In fact it is the antithesis of reading. Briefing is terse, factual and to the point. Reading is untidy, discursive and perpetually inviting. Briefing closes down a subject, reading opens it up.'

'I wonder whether I can bring Your Majesty back to the visit to the shoe factory,' said Sir Kevin.

'Next time,' said the Queen shortly. 'Where did I put my book?'

HAVING DISCOVERED the delights of reading herself, Her Majesty was keen to pass them on.

'Do you read, Summers?' she said to the chauffeur en route for Northampton.

'Read, ma'am?'

'Books?'

'When I get the chance, ma'am. I never seem to find the time.'

'That's what a lot of people say. One must make the time. Take this morning. You're going to be sitting outside the town hall waiting for me. You could read then.'

'I have to watch the motor, ma'am. This is the Midlands. Vandalism is universal.'

With Her Majesty safely delivered into the hands of the lord lieutenant, Summers did a precautionary circuit of the motor, then settled down in his seat. Read? Of course he read. Everybody read. He opened the glove compartment and took out his copy of the *Sun*.

Others, notably Norman, were more sympathetic, and from him she made no attempt to hide her shortcomings as a reader or her lack of cultural credentials altogether.

'Do you know,' she said one afternoon as they were reading in her study, 'do you know the area in which one would truly excel?'

'No, ma'am?'

'The pub quiz. One has been everywhere, seen everything and though one might have difficulty with pop music and some sport, when it comes to the capital of Zimbabwe, say, or the principal exports of New South Wales, I have all that at my fingertips.'

'And I could do the pop,' said Norman.

'Yes,' said the Queen. 'We would make a good team. Ah well. The road not travelled. Who's that?'

'Who, ma'am?'

'The road not travelled. Look it up.'

Norman looked it up in the *Dictionary of Quotations* to find that it was Robert Frost.

'I know the word for you,' said the Queen.

'Ma'am?'

'You run errands, you change my library books, you look up awkward words in the dictionary and find me quotations. Do you know what you are?'

'I used to be a skivvy, ma'am.'

'Well, you're not a skivvy now. You're my amanuensis.'

Norman looked it up in the dictionary the Queen now kept always on her desk. 'One who writes from dictation, copies manuscripts. A literary assistant.'

The new amanuensis had a chair in the corridor, handy for the Queen's office, on which, when he was not on call or running errands, he would spend his time reading. This did him no good at all with the other pages, who thought he was on a cushy number and not comely enough to deserve it. Occasionally a passing equerry would stop and ask him if he had nothing better to do than read, and to begin with he had been stuck for a reply. Nowadays, though, he said he was reading something for Her Majesty, which was often true but was also satisfactorily irritating and so sent the equerry away in a bad temper.

READING MORE and more, the Queen now drew her books from various libraries, including some of her own, but for sentimental reasons and because she liked Mr Hutchings, she still occasionally made a trip down to the kitchen yard to patronise the travelling library.

One Wednesday afternoon, though, it wasn't there, nor the following week either. Norman was straightaway on the case, only to be told that the visit to the palace had been cancelled due to all-round cutbacks. Undeterred, Norman eventually tracked the library down to Pimlico, where in a schoolyard he found Mr Hutchings still doggedly at the wheel, sticking labels on the books. Mr Hutchings told him that though he had pointed out to the Libraries Outreach Department that Her Majesty was one of their borrowers this cut no ice with the council, which, prior to axing the visits, said that inquiries had been made at the palace and it had disclaimed any interest in the matter.

Told this by the outraged Norman, the Queen seemed unsurprised, but though she said nothing to him it confirmed what she had suspected, namely that in royal circles reading, or at any rate her reading, was not well looked on.

Small setback though the loss of the travelling library was, there was one happy outcome, as Mr Hutchings found himself figuring on the next honours list; it was, admittedly, in quite a lowly capacity, but numbered among those who had done Her Majesty some special and personal service. This was not well looked on either, particularly by Sir Kevin.

Since he was from New Zealand and something of a departure when he was appointed, Sir Kevin Scatchard had inevitably been hailed in the press as a new broom, a young(ish) man who would sweep away some of the redundant deference and more flagrant flummeries that were monarchy's customary accretions, the Crown in this version pictured as not unlike Miss Havisham's wedding feast – the cobwebbed chandeliers, the mice-infested cake and Sir

Kevin as Mr Pip tearing down the rotting curtains to let in the light. The Queen, who had the advantage of having once been a breath of fresh air herself, was unconvinced by this scenario, suspecting that this brisk Antipodean wind would in due course blow itself out. Private secretaries, like prime ministers, came and went, and in Sir Kevin's case the Queen felt she might simply be a stepping stone to those corporate heights for which he was undoubtedly headed. He was a graduate of the Harvard Business School and one of his publicly stated aims ('setting out our stall', as he put it) was to make the monarchy more accessible. The opening of Buckingham Palace to visitors had been a step down this road, as was the use of the garden for occasional concerts, pop and otherwise. The reading, though, made him uneasy.

'I feel, ma'am, that while not exactly elitist it sends the wrong message. It tends to exclude.'

'Exclude? Surely most people can read?'

'They can read, ma'am, but I'm not sure that they do.'

'Then, Sir Kevin, I am setting them a good example.'

She smiled sweetly, while noting that these days Sir Kevin was much less of a New Zealander than when he had first been appointed, his accent now with only a tincture of that Kiwi connection about which Her Majesty knew he was sensitive and of which he did not wish to be reminded (Norman had told her).

Another delicate issue was his name. The private secretary felt burdened by his name: Kevin was not the name he would have chosen for himself and disliking it made him more aware of the number of times the Queen used it, though she could hardly have been aware of how demeaning he felt it.

In fact she knew perfectly well (Norman again), but to her everybody's name was immaterial, as indeed was everything else, their clothes, their voice, their class. She was a genuine democrat, perhaps the only one in the country.

To Sir Kevin, though, it seemed that she used his name unnecessarily often, and there were times when he was sure she gave it a breath of New Zealand, that land of sheep and Sunday afternoons, and a country which, as head of the Commonwealth, she had several times visited and claimed to be enthusiastic about.

'It's important', said Sir Kevin, 'that Your Majesty should stay focused.'

'When you say "stay focused", Sir Kevin, I suppose you mean one should keep one's eye on the ball. Well, I've had my eye on the ball for more than fifty years so I think these days one is allowed the occasional glance to the boundary.' She felt that her metaphor had probably slipped a little there, not, though, that Sir Kevin noticed.

'I can understand', he said, 'Your Majesty's need to pass the time.'

'Pass the time?' said the Queen. 'Books are not about passing the time. They're about other lives. Other worlds. Far from wanting time to pass, Sir Kevin, one just wishes one had more of it. If one wanted to pass the time one could go to New Zealand.'

With two mentions of his name and one of New Zealand Sir Kevin retired hurt. Still, he had made a point and he would have been gratified to know that it left the Queen troubled, and wondering why it was that at this particular time in her life she had suddenly felt the pull of books. Where had this appetite come from?

Few people, after all, had seen more of the world than she had. There was scarcely a country she had not visited, a notability she had not met. Herself part of the panoply of the world, why now was she intrigued by books which, whatever else they might be, were just a reflection of the world or a version of it? Books? She had seen the real thing.

'I read, I think,' she said to Norman, 'because one has a duty to find out what people are like,' a trite enough remark of which Norman took not much notice, feeling himself under no such obligation and reading purely for pleasure, not enlightenment, though part of the pleasure was the enlightenment, he could see that. But duty did not come into it.

To someone with the background of the Queen, though, pleasure had always taken second place to duty. If she could feel she had a duty to read then she could set about it with a clear conscience, with the pleasure, if pleasure there was, incidental. But why did it take possession of her now? This she did not discuss with Norman, as she felt it had to do with who she was and the position she occupied.

The appeal of reading, she thought, lay in its indifference: there was something lofty about literature. Books did not care who was reading them or whether one read them or not. All readers were equal, herself included. Literature, she thought, is a common-wealth; letters a republic. Actually she had heard this phrase, the republic of letters, used before, at graduation ceremonies, honorary degrees and the like, though without knowing quite what it meant. At that time talk of a republic of any sort she had thought mildly insulting and in her actual presence tactless to say the least. It was only now she understood what it meant. Books did not defer. All readers were equal, and this took her back to the beginning of her life. As a girl, one of her greatest thrills had been on VE night, when she and her sister had slipped out of the gates and mingled unrecognised with the crowds. There was something of that, she felt, to reading. It was anonymous; it was shared; it was common. And she who had led a life apart now found that she craved it. Here in these pages and between these covers she could go unrecognised.

These doubts and self-questionings, though, were just the beginning. Once she got into her stride it ceased to seem strange to her that she wanted to read, and books, to which she had taken so cautiously, gradually came to be her element.

ONE OF THE Queen's recurrent royal responsibilities was to open Parliament, an obligation she had never previously found particularly burdensome and actually rather enjoyed: to be driven down the Mall on a bright autumn morning even after fifty years was something of a treat. But not any more. She was dreading the two hours the whole thing was due to take, though fortunately they were in the coach, not the open carriage, so she could take along her book. She'd got quite good at reading and waving, the trick being to keep the book below the level of the window and to keep focused on it and not on the crowds. The duke didn't like it one bit, of course, but goodness it helped.

Which was all very well, except it was only when she was actually in the coach, with the procession drawn up in the palace forecourt and ready for the off, that, as she put on her glasses, she realised she'd forgotten the book. And while the duke fumes in the corner and the postillions fidget, the horses shift and the harness clinks, Norman is rung on the mobile. The Guardsmen stand at ease and the procession waits. The officer in charge looks at his watch. Two minutes late. Knowing nothing displeases Her Majesty more and knowing nothing of the book, he does not look forward to the repercussions that must inevitably follow. But here is Norman, skittering across the gravel with the book thoughtfully hidden in a shawl, and off they go.

Still, it is an ill-tempered royal couple that is driven down the Mall, the duke waving viciously from his side, the Queen listlessly from hers, and at some speed, too, as the procession tries to pick up the two minutes that have been lost.

At Westminster she popped the offending book behind a cushion in the carriage ready for the journey back, mindful as she sat on the throne and embarked on her speech of how tedious was the twaddle she was called on to deliver and that this was actually the only occasion when she got to read aloud to the nation. 'My government will do this . . . my government will do that.' It was so barbarously phrased and wholly devoid of style or interest that she felt it demeaned the very act of reading itself, with this year's performance even more garbled than usual as she, too, tried to pick up the missing couple of minutes.

It was with some relief that she got back into the coach and reached behind the cushion for her book. It was not there. Steadfastly waving as they rumbled along, she surreptitiously felt behind the other cushions.

'You're not sitting on it?'

'Sitting on what?'

'My book.'

'No, I am not. Some British Legion people here, and wheelchairs. Wave, for God's sake.'

When they arrived at the palace she had a word with Grant, the young footman in charge, who said that while ma'am had been in the Lords the sniffer dogs had been round and security had confiscated the book. He thought it had probably been exploded.

'Exploded?' said the Queen. 'But it was Anita Brookner.'

The young man, who seemed remarkably undeferential, said security may have thought it was a device.

The Queen said: 'Yes. That is exactly what it is. A book is a device to ignite the imagination.'

The footman said: 'Yes, ma'am.'

It was as if he was talking to his grandmother, and

not for the first time the Queen was made unpleas-
antly aware of the hostility her reading seemed to
arouse.

'Very well,' she said. 'Then you should inform
security that I shall expect to find another copy of the
same book, vetted and explosive-free, waiting on my
desk tomorrow morning. And another thing. The
carriage cushions are filthy. Look at my gloves.' Her
Majesty departed.

'Fuck,' said the footman, fishing out the book
from where he had been told to hide it down the
front of his breeches. But of the lateness of the procession, to everyone's surprise nothing was officially
said.

This dislike of the Queen's reading was not confined to the household. Whereas in the past walkies
had meant a noisy and unrestrained romp in the
grounds, these days, once she was out of sight of the
house Her Majesty sank onto the nearest seat and
took out her book. Occasionally she threw a bored
biscuit in the direction of the dogs, but there was
none of that ball-throwing, stick-fetching and
orchestrated frenzy that used to enliven their peram-
bulations. Indulged and bad-tempered though they

were, the dogs were not unintelligent, so it was not surprising that in a short space of time they came to hate books as the spoilsports they were (and always have been).

Did Her Majesty ever let a book fall to the carpet it would straightaway be leaped on by any attendant dog, worried and slavered over and borne to the distant reaches of the palace or wherever so that it could be satisfyingly torn apart. The James Tait Black prize notwithstanding, Ian McEwan had ended up like this and even A. S. Byatt. Patron of the London Library though she was, Her Majesty regularly found herself on the phone apologising to the renewals clerk for the loss of yet another volume.

The dogs disliked Norman, too, and in so far as the young man could be blamed for some at least of the Queen's literary enthusiasm, Sir Kevin didn't care for him either. He was also irritated by his constant proximity because, while he was never actually in the room when the private secretary talked to the Queen, he was always within call.

They were discussing a royal visit to Wales due to take place in a fortnight's time. In the middle of being taken through her programme (a ride on a super-tram, a ukulele concert and a tour round a cheese factory), Her Majesty suddenly got up and went to the door.

'Norman.'

Sir Kevin heard a chair scrape as Norman got up.

'We're going to Wales in a few weeks' time.'

'Bad luck, ma'am.'

The Queen smiled back at the unsmiling Sir Kevin.

'Norman is so cheeky. Now we've read Dylan Thomas, haven't we, and some John Cowper Powys. And Jan Morris we've read. But who else is there?'

'You could try Kilvert, ma'am,' said Norman.

'Who's he?'

'A vicar, ma'am. Nineteenth century. Lived on the Welsh borders and wrote a diary. Fond of little girls.'

'Oh,' said the Queen, 'like Lewis Carroll.'

'Worse, ma'am.'

'Dear me. Can you get me the diaries?'

'I'll add them to our list, ma'am.'

Her Majesty closed the door and came back to her desk. 'You see, you can't say I don't do my homework, Sir Kevin.'

Sir Kevin, who had never heard of Kilvert, was

unimpressed. 'The cheese factory is in a new business park, sited on reclaimed colliery land. It's revitalised the whole area.'

'Oh, I'm sure,' said the Queen. 'But you must admit that the literature is relevant.'

'I don't know that it is,' said Sir Kevin. 'The next-door factory where Your Majesty is opening the canteen makes computer components.'

'Some singing, I suppose?' said the Queen.

'There will be a choir, ma'am.'

'There generally is.'

Sir Kevin had a very muscular face, the Queen thought. He seemed to have muscles in his cheeks and when he frowned, they rippled. If she were a novelist, she thought, that might be worth writing down.

'We must make sure, ma'am, that we're singing from the same hymn sheet.'

'In Wales, yes. Most certainly. Any news from home? Busy shearing away?'

'Not at this time of year, ma'am.'

'Oh. Out to grass.'

She smiled the wide smile that indicated that the interview was over and when he turned to bow his head at the door she was already back in her book and without looking up simply murmured 'Sir Kevin' and turned the page.

So IN DUE course Her Majesty went to Wales and to Scotland and to Lancashire and the West Country in that unremitting round of nationwide perambulation that is the lot of the monarch. The Queen must meet her people, however awkward and tongue-tied such meetings might turn out to be. Though it was here that her staff could help.

To get round the occasional speechlessness of her subjects when confronted with their sovereign the equerries would sometimes proffer handy hints as to possible conversations.

'Her Majesty may well ask you if you have had far to come. Have your answer ready and then possibly go on to say whether you came by train or by car. She may then ask you where you have left the car and whether the traffic was busier here than in – where did you say you came from? – Andover. The Queen, you see, is interested in all aspects of the nation's life, so she will sometimes talk about how difficult it is to park in London these days, which could take you on to a discussion of any parking problems you might have in Basingstoke.'

'Andover, actually, though Basingstoke's a nightmare too.'

'Quite so. But you get the idea? Small talk.'

Mundane though these conversations might be they had the merit of being predictable and above all brief, affording Her Majesty plenty of opportunities to cut the exchange short. The encounters ran smoothly and to a schedule, the Queen seemed interested and her subjects were seldom at a loss, and that perhaps the most eagerly anticipated conversation of their lives had only amounted to a discussion of the coned-off sections of the M6 hardly mattered. They had met the Queen and she had spoken to them and everyone got away on time.

So routine had such exchanges become that the equerries now scarcely bothered to invigilate them, hovering on the outskirts of the gathering always with a helpful if condescending smile. So it was only when it became plain that the tongue-tied quotient was increasing and that more and more of her subjects were at a loss when talking to Her Majesty that the staff began to eavesdrop on what was (or was not) being said.

It transpired that with no prior notification to her attendants the Queen had abandoned her long-standing lines of inquiry – length of service, distance travelled, place of origin – and had embarked on a new conversational gambit, namely, 'What are you reading at the moment?' To this very few of Her Majesty's loyal subjects had a ready answer (though one did try: 'The Bible?'). Hence the awkward pauses which the Queen tended to fill by saying, 'I'm reading . . .', sometimes even fishing in her handbag and giving them a glimpse of the lucky volume. Unsurprisingly the audiences got longer and more ragged, with a growing number of her loving subjects going away regretting that they had not performed well and feeling, too, that the monarch had somehow bowled them a googly.

Off duty, Piers, Tristram, Giles and Elspeth, all the Queen's devoted servants, compare notes: 'What are you reading? I mean, what sort of question is that? Most people, poor dears, aren't reading anything. Except if they say that, madam roots in her handbag, fetches out some volume she's just finished and makes them a present of it.'

'Which they promptly sell on eBay.'

'Quite. And have you been on a royal visit recently?' one of the ladies-in-waiting chips in. 'Because the word has got round. Whereas once upon a time the dear people would fetch along the odd daffodil or a bunch of mouldy old primroses which Her Majesty then passed back to us bringing up the rear, nowadays they fetch along books they're reading, or, wait for it, even writing, and if you're unlucky enough to be in attendance you practically need a trolley. If I'd wanted to cart books around I'd have got a job in Hatchards. I'm afraid Her Majesty is getting to be what is known as a handful.'

Still, the equerries accommodated, and disgruntled though they were at having to vary their routine, in the light of the Queen's new predilection her attendants reluctantly changed tack and in their pre-presentation warm-up now suggested that while Her Majesty might, as of old, still inquire as to how far the presentee had come and by what means, these days she was more likely to ask what the person was currently reading.

At this most people looked blank (and sometimes

panic-stricken) but, nothing daunted, the equerries came up with a list of suggestions. Though this meant that the Queen came away with a disproportionate notion of the popularity of Andy McNab and the near universal affection for Joanna Trollope, no matter; at least embarrassment had been avoided. And once the answers had been supplied the audiences were back on track and finished on the dot as they used to do, the only hold-ups when, as seldom, one of her subjects confessed to a fondness for Virginia Woolf or Dickens, both of which provoked a lively (and lengthy) discussion. There were many who hoped for a similar meeting of minds by saying they were reading Harry Potter, but to this the Queen (who had no time for fantasy) invariably said briskly, 'Yes. One is saving that for a rainy day,' and passed swiftly on.

Seeing her almost daily meant that Sir Kevin was able to nag the Queen about what was now almost an obsession and to devise different approaches. 'I was wondering, ma'am, if we could somehow factor in your reading.' Once she would have let this pass, but one effect of reading had been to diminish the Queen's tolerance for jargon (which had always been low).

'Factor it in? What does that mean?'

'I'm just kicking the tyres on this one, ma'am, but it would help if we were able to put out a press release saying that, apart from English literature, Your Majesty was also reading ethnic classics.'

'Which ethnic classics did you have in mind, Sir Kevin? The Kama Sutra?'

Sir Kevin sighed.

'I am reading Vikram Seth at the moment. Would he count?'

Though the private secretary had never heard of him he thought he sounded right.

'Salman Rushdie?'

'Probably not, ma'am.'

'I don't see', said the Queen, 'why there is any need for a press release at all. Why should the public care what I am reading? The Queen reads. That is all they need to know. "So what?" I imagine the general response.'

'To read is to withdraw. To make oneself unavailable. One would feel easier about it', said Sir Kevin, 'if the pursuit itself were less . . . selfish.'

'Selfish?'

'Perhaps I should say solipsistic.'

'Perhaps you should.'

Sir Kevin plunged on. 'Were we able to harness your reading to some larger purpose – the literacy of the nation as a whole, for instance, the improvement of reading standards among the young . . .'

'One reads for pleasure,' said the Queen. 'It is not a public duty.'

'Perhaps', said Sir Kevin, 'it should be.'

'Bloody cheek,' said the duke when she told him that night.

APROPOS THE duke, what of the family in all this? How did the Queen's reading impinge on them?

Had it been Her Majesty's responsibility to prepare meals, to shop or, unimaginably, to dust and hoover the house(s), standards would straightaway have been perceived to have fallen. But, of course, she had to do none of these things. That she did her boxes with less assiduity is true, but this didn't affect her husband or her children. What it did affect (or 'impact upon', as Sir Kevin put it) was the public sphere, where she had begun to perform her duties with a perceived reluctance: she laid foundation stones with less élan and what few ships there were to launch she sent down the slipway with no more ceremony than a toy boat on a pond, her book always waiting.

While this might concern her staff, her family were actually rather relieved. She had always kept them up to the mark and age had not made her more indulgent. Reading, though, had. She left the family more to themselves, chivvied them hardly at all and they had an easier time altogether. Hurray for books was their feeling, except when they were required to read them or when grandmama insisted on talking about them, quizzing them about their own reading habits or, worst of all, pressing books into their hands and checking later to see if they had been read.

As it was, they would often come upon her in odd unfrequented corners of her various dwellings, spectacles on the end of her nose, notebook and pencil beside her. She would glance up briefly and raise a vague, acknowledging hand. 'Well, I'm glad somebody's happy,' said the duke as he shuffled off down the corridor. And it was true; she was. She enjoyed reading like nothing else and devoured books at an astonishing rate, not that, Norman apart, there was anyone to be astonished.

Nor initially did she discuss her reading with anyone, least of all in public, knowing that such a late-flowering enthusiasm, however worthwhile, might expose her to ridicule. It would be the same, she thought, if she had developed a passion for God, or dahlias. At her age, people thought, why bother? To her, though, nothing could have been more serious, and she felt about reading what some writers felt about writing, that it was impossible not to do it and that at this late stage of her life she had been chosen to read as others were chosen to write.

To begin with, it's true, she read with trepidation and some unease. The sheer endlessness of books outfaced her and she had no idea how to go on; there was no system to her reading, with one book leading to another, and often she had two or three on the go at the same time. The next stage had been when she started to make notes, after which she always read with a pencil in hand, not summarising what she read but simply transcribing passages that struck her. It was only after a year or so of reading and making notes that she tentatively ventured on the occasional thought of her own. 'I think of literature', she wrote, 'as a vast country to the far borders of which I am journeying but cannot possibly reach. And I have started too late. I will never catch up.' Then (an unrelated thought): 'Etiquette may be bad but embarrassment is worse.'

There was sadness to her reading, too, and for the first time in her life she felt there was a good deal she had missed. She had been reading one of the several lives of Sylvia Plath and was actually quite happy to have missed most of that, but reading the memoirs of Lauren Bacall she could not help feeling that Ms Bacall had had a much better bite at the carrot and, slightly to her surprise, found herself envying her for it.

That the Queen could readily switch from showbiz autobiography to the last days of a suicidal poet might seem both incongruous and wanting in perception. But, certainly in her early days, to her all books were the same and, as with her subjects, she felt a duty to approach them without prejudice. For her, there was no such thing as an improving book. Books were uncharted country and, to begin with at any rate, she made no distinction between them.

With time came discrimination, but apart from the occasional word from Norman, nobody told her what to read, and what not. Lauren Bacall, Winifred Holtby, Sylvia Plath – who were they? Only by reading could she find out.

It was a few weeks later that she looked up from her book and said to Norman: 'Do you know that I said you were my amanuensis? Well, I've discovered what I am. I am an opsimath.'

With the dictionary always to hand, Norman read out: 'Opsimath: one who learns only late in life.'

It was this sense of making up for lost time that made her read with such rapidity and in the process now adding more frequent (and more confident) comments of her own, bringing to what was in effect literary criticism the same forthrightness with which she tackled other departments of her life. She was not a gentle reader and often wished authors were around so that she could take them to task.

'Am I alone', she wrote, 'in wanting to give Henry James a good talking-to?'

'I can see why Dr Johnson is well thought of, but surely, much of it is opinionated rubbish?'

It was Henry James she was reading one teatime

when she said out loud, 'Oh, do get on.'

The maid, who was just taking away the tea trolley, said, 'Sorry, ma'am,' and shot out of the room in two seconds flat.

'Not you, Alice,' the Queen called after her, even going to the door. 'Not you.'

Previously she wouldn't have cared what the maid thought or that she might have hurt her feelings, only now she did and coming back to the chair she wondered why. That this access of consideration might have something to do with books and even with the perpetually irritating Henry James did not at that moment occur to her.

Though the awareness of all the catching up she had to do never left her, her other regret was to do with all the famous authors she could have met but hadn't. In this respect at least she could mend her ways and she decided, partly at Norman's urging, that it would be interesting and even fun to meet some of the authors they had both been reading. Accordingly a reception was arranged, or a soirée, as Norman insisted on calling it.

The equerries naturally expected that the same form would apply as at the garden parties and other large receptions, with the tipping off of guests to whom Her Majesty was likely to stop and talk. The Queen, though, thought that on this occasion such formality was misplaced (these were artists after all) and decided to take pot luck. This turned out not to be a good idea.

Shy and even timid though authors had generally seemed to be when she had met them individually, taken together they were loud, gossipy and, though they laughed a good deal, not, so far as she could tell, particularly funny. She found herself hovering on the edge of groups, with no one making much effort to include her, so that she felt like a guest at her own party. And when she did speak she either killed conversation and plunged it into an awful pause or the authors, presumably to demonstrate their independence and sophistication, took no notice at all of what she said and just went on talking.

It was exciting to be with writers she had come to think of as her friends and whom she longed to know. But now, when she was aching to declare her fellow feeling with those whose books she had read and admired, she found she had nothing to say. She, who had seldom in her life been intimidated by anyone, now found herself tongue-tied and awkward. 'I adored your book,' would have said it all, but fifty years of composure and self-possession plus half a century of understatement stood in the way. Hard put for conversation, she found herself falling back on some of her stock stand-bys. It wasn't quite 'How far did you have to come?' but their literary equivalent. 'How do you think of your characters? Do you work regular hours? Do you use a word-processor?' – questions which she knew were clichés and were embarrassing to inflict had the awkward silence not been worse.

One Scottish author was particularly alarming. Asked where his inspiration came from, he said fiercely: 'It doesn't come, Your Majesty. You have to go out and fetch it.'

When she did manage to express – and almost stammer – her admiration, hoping the author would tell her how he (the men, she decided, much worse than the women) had come to write the book in question, she found her enthusiasm brushed aside, as he insisted on talking not about the bestseller he had just written but about the one on which he was currently at work and how slowly it was going and how in consequence, as he sipped his champagne, he was the most miserable of creatures.

Authors, she soon decided, were probably best met with in the pages of their novels, and were as much creatures of the reader's imagination as the characters in their books. Nor did they seem to think one had done them a kindness by reading their writings. Rather they had done one the kindness by writing them.

To begin with she had thought she might hold such gatherings on a regular basis, but this soirée was enough to disabuse her of that. Once was enough. This came as a relief to Sir Kevin, who had not been enthusiastic, pointing out that if ma'am held an evening for the writers she would then have to hold a similar evening for the artists, and having held evenings for writers and artists the scientists would then expect to be entertained, too.

'Ma'am must not be seen to be partial.'

Well, there was now no danger of that.

With some justification, Sir Kevin blamed Norman for this evening of literary lacklustre, as he had encouraged the Queen when she had tentatively mentioned the idea. It wasn't as if Norman had had much of a time either. Literature being what it is the gay quotient among the guests was quite high, some of them asked along at Norman's specific suggestion. Not that that did him any good at all. Though like the other pages he was just taking round the drinks and the nibbles that went with them, Norman knew, as the others didn't, the reputation and standing of those whom he was bobbing up to with his tray. He had even read their books. But it was not Norman around whom they clustered, but the dolly pages and the loftier equerries who, as Norman said bitterly (though not to the Queen), wouldn't know a literary reputation if they stepped in it.

Still, if the whole experience of entertaining the Living Word was unfortunate, it did not (as Sir Kevin had hoped) put Her Majesty off reading. It turned her off wanting to meet authors, and to some extent off living authors altogether. But this just meant that she had more time for the classics, for Dickens, Thackeray, George Eliot and the Brontës.

EVERY TUESDAY evening the Queen saw her prime minister, who briefed her on what he felt she ought to know. The press were fond of picturing these meetings as those of a wise and experienced monarch guiding her first minister past possible pitfalls and drawing on her unique repository of political experience accumulated over the fifty-odd years she had been on the throne in order to give him advice. This was a myth, though one in which the palace itself collaborated, the truth being the longer they were in office the less the prime ministers listened and the more they talked, the Queen nodding assent though not always agreement.

To begin with prime ministers wanted the Queen to hold their hand, and when they came to see her it was to be stroked and given an approving pat in the spirit of a child wanting to show its mother what it has done. And, as so often with her, it was really a show that was required, a show of interest, a show of concern. Men (and this included Mrs Thatcher) wanted show. At this stage, though, they still listened and even asked her advice, but as time passed all her prime ministers modulated with disturbing similarity into lecturing mode, when they ceased to require encouragement from the Queen but treated her like an audience, listening to her no longer on the agenda.

It was not only Gladstone who addressed the Queen as if she was a public meeting.

The audience this particular Tuesday had followed the usual pattern, and it was only when it was drawing to a close that the Queen managed to get a word in and talk about a subject that actually interested her. 'About my Christmas broadcast.'

'Yes, ma'am?' said the prime minister.

'I thought this year one might do something different.'

'Different, ma'am?'

'Yes. If one were to be sitting on a sofa reading or, even more informally, be discovered by the camera curled up with a book, the camera could creep in – is that the expression? – until I'm in mid-shot, when I could look up and say, "I've been reading this book about such and such," and then go on from there.'

'And what would the book be, ma'am?' The prime minister looked unhappy.

'That one would have to think about.'

'Something about the state of the world perhaps?' He brightened.

'Possibly, though they get quite enough of that from

the newspapers. No. I was actually thinking of poetry.'

'Poetry, ma'am?' He smiled thinly.

'Thomas Hardy, for instance. I read an awfully good poem of his the other day about how the *Titanic* and the iceberg that was to sink her came together. It's called "The Convergence of the Twain". Do you know it?'

'I don't, ma'am. But how would it help?'

'Help whom?'

'Well' – and the prime minister seemed a trifle embarrassed actually to have to say it – 'the people.'

'Oh, surely', said the Queen, 'it would show, wouldn't it, that fate is something to which we are all subject.'

She gazed at the prime minister, smiling helpfully. He looked down at his hands.

'I'm not sure that is a message the government would feel able to endorse.' The public must not be allowed to think the world could not be managed. That way lay chaos. Or defeat at the polls, which was the same thing.

'I'm told' – and now it was his turn to smile helpfully – 'that there is some excellent footage of Your Majesty's visit to South Africa.'

The Queen sighed and pressed the bell. 'We will think about it.'

The prime minister knew that the audience was over as Norman opened the door and waited. 'So this', thought the prime minister, 'is the famous Norman.'

'Oh, Norman,' said the Queen, 'the prime minister doesn't seem to have read Hardy. Perhaps you could find him one of our old paperbacks on his way out.'

Slightly to her surprise the Queen did after a fashion get her way, and though she was not curled up on the sofa but seated at her usual table, and though she did not read the Hardy poem (rejected as not 'forward-looking'), she began her Christmas broadcast with the opening paragraph of *A Tale of Two Cities* ('It was the best of times. It was the worst of times') and did it well, too. Choosing not to read from the autocue but from the book itself, she reminded the older ones in her audience (and they were the majority) of the kind of teacher some of them could still remember and who had read to them at school.

Encouraged by the reception given to her Christmas broadcast she persisted with her notion of reading in public, and late one night, as she closed her book on the Elizabethan Settlement, it occurred to her to ring the Archbishop of Canterbury.

There was a pause while he turned down the TV.

'Archbishop. Why do I never read the lesson?'

'I beg your pardon, ma'am?'

'In church. Everybody else gets to read and one never does. It's not laid down, is it? It's not off-limits?'

'Not that I'm aware, ma'am.'

'Good. Well in that case I'm going to start. Leviticus, here I come. Goodnight.'

The archbishop shook his head and went back to *Strictly Come Dancing*.

But thereafter, particularly when she was in Norfolk, and even in Scotland, Her Majesty began to do a regular stint at the lectern. And not merely the lectern. Visiting a Norfolk primary school she sat down on a classroom chair and read a story from Babar to the children. Addressing a City banquet she treated them to a Betjeman poem, impromptu departures from her schedule which enchanted everyone except Sir Kevin, from whom she hadn't bothered to get clearance.

Also unscheduled was the conclusion of a tree-planting ceremony. Having lightly dug an oak sapling into the reclaimed earth of a bleak urban farm above the Medway, she rested on the ceremonial spade and recited by heart Philip Larkin's poem 'The Trees', with its final verse:

> Yet still the unresting castles thresh
> In fullgrown thickness every May.
> Last year is dead, they seem to say,
> Begin afresh, afresh, afresh.

And as that clear and unmistakable voice carried over the shabby wind-bitten grass it seemed it was not just the huddled municipal party she was addressing but herself too. It was her life she was calling upon, the new beginning hers.

Still, though reading absorbed her, what the Queen had not expected was the degree to which it drained her of enthusiasm for anything else. It's true that at the prospect of opening yet another swimming-baths her heart didn't exactly leap up, but even so, she had never actually resented having to do it. However tedious her obligations had been – visiting this, conferring that – boredom had never come into it. This was her duty and when she opened her engagement book every morning it had never been without interest or expectation.

No more. Now she surveyed the unrelenting pro-gression of tours, travels and undertakings stretching years into the future only with dread. There was scarcely a day she could call her own and never two. Suddenly it had all become a drag. 'Ma'am is tired,' said her maid, hearing her groan at her desk. 'It's time ma'am put her feet up occasionally.'

But it wasn't that. It was reading, and love it though she did, there were times when she wished she had never opened a book and entered into other lives. It had spoiled her. Or spoiled her for this, anyway.

MEANWHILE the grand visitors came and went, one of them the president of France who proved such a let-down on the Genet front. She mentioned this to the foreign secretary in the debriefing that was customary after such visits, but he had never heard of the convict-playwright either. Still, she said, drifting rather from the comments the president had made about Anglo-French monetary arrangements, dead loss though he had been on Genet (whom he had dismissed as 'a denizen of the billiard hall'), he had proved a mine of information about Proust, who had hitherto just been a name to the Queen. To the foreign secretary he was not even that, and so she was able to fill him in a little.

'Terrible life, poor man. A martyr to asthma, apparently, and really someone to whom one would have wanted to say, "Oh do pull your socks up." But literature's full of those. The curious thing about him was that when he dipped his cake in his tea (disgusting habit) the whole of his past life came back to him. Well, I tried it and it had no effect on me at all. The real treat when I was a child was Fuller's cakes. I suppose it might work with me if I were to taste one of them, but of course they've long since gone out of business, so no memories there. Are we finished?' She reached for her book.

The Queen's ignorance of Proust was, unlike the foreign secretary's, soon to be remedied, as Norman straightaway looked him up on the internet and, finding that the novel ran to thirteen volumes, thought it would be ideal reading on Her Majesty's summer holiday at Balmoral. George Painter's biography of Proust went with them, too. And seeing the blue- and pink-jacketed volumes ranged along her desk, the Queen thought they looked almost edible and straight out of a patisserie window.

It was a foul summer, cold, wet and unproductive, the guns grumbling every evening at their paltry bag. But for the Queen (and for Norman) it was an idyll. Seldom can there have been more of a contrast between the world of the book and the place in which it was read, the pair of them engrossed in the sufferings of Swann, the petty vulgarities of Mme Verdurin and the absurdities of Baron de Charlus, while in the wet butts on the hills the guns cracked out their empty tattoo and the occasional dead and sodden stag was borne past the window.

Duty required that the prime minister and his wife join the house party for a few days, and though not a shot himself he was at least hoping to accompany the Queen on some brisk walks through the heather where, as he put it, he 'hoped to get to know her better'. But knowing less of Proust than he did even of Thomas Hardy, the prime minister was disappointed: these would-be heart-to-hearts were never on the cards.

Breakfast over, Her Majesty retired to her study

with Norman, the men drove off in their Land Rovers for another disappointing day and the prime minister and his wife were left to their own devices. Some days they trailed through the heather and over the moors to eat a wet and awkward picnic with the guns, but in the afternoon, having exhausted the area's shopping potential by buying a tweed rug and a box of short-bread, they could be found in a distant corner of the drawing room playing a sad game of Monopoly.

Four days of this was enough, and making an excuse ('trouble in the Middle East') the prime minister and his lady determined to depart early. On their last evening a game of charades was hurriedly organised, the choice of each well-known phrase or saying apparently one of the lesser-known prerogatives of the monarch, and well known though they may have been to her, they were a mystery to everyone else, including the prime minister.

The prime minister never liked to lose, even to the monarch, and it was no consolation to be told by one of the princes that no one but the Queen could hope to win, as the questions (several of them about Proust) were set by Norman and taken from their reading.

Had Her Majesty resumed a raft of long-disused prerogatives the prime minister could not have been more put out, and on his return to London he wasted no time in getting his special adviser on to Sir Kevin, who condoled with him, while pointing out that currently Norman was a burden they all had to share. The special adviser was unimpressed. 'Is this bloke Norman a nancy?'

Sir Kevin didn't know for certain but thought it was possible.

'And does she know that?'

'Her Majesty? Probably.'

'And do the press?'

'I think the press', said Sir Kevin, clenching and unclenching his cheeks, 'are the last thing we want.'

'Exactly. So can I leave it with you?'

It happened that upcoming was a state visit to Canada, a treat that Norman was not down to share, preferring to go home for his holidays to Stockton-on-Tees. However, he made all the preparations beforehand, carefully packing a case of books that would see Her Majesty fully occupied from coast to farthest coast. The Canadians were not, so far as Norman knew, a bookish people and the schedule was so tight that the chances of Her Majesty getting to browse in a bookshop were slim. She was looking forward to the trip, as much of the journey was by train, and she pictured herself in happy seclusion whisked across the continent as she turned the pages of Pepys, whom she was reading for the first time.

In fact, though, the tour, or at least the beginning of it, turned out to be disastrous. The Queen was bored, uncooperative and glum, shortcomings all of which her equerries would readily have blamed on her reading, were it not for the fact that, on this occasion, she had no reading, the books Norman had packed for her having unaccountably gone missing. Dispatched from Heathrow with the royal party, they turned up months later in Calgary, where they were made the focus of a nice if rather eccentric exhibition at the local library. In the meantime, though, Her Majesty had nothing to occupy her mind and rather than focusing her attention on the job in hand, which had been Sir Kevin's intention in arranging for the books' misdirection, being at a loose end just made her bad-tempered and difficult.

In the far north what few polar bears could be

assembled hung about waiting for Her Majesty, but when she did not appear loped off to an ice floe that held more promise. Logs jammed, glaciers slid into the freezing waters, all unobserved by the royal visitor, who kept to her cabin.

'Don't you want to look at the St Lawrence Seaway?' said her husband.

'I opened it fifty years ago. I don't suppose it's changed.'

Even the Rockies received only a perfunctory glance and Niagara Falls was given a miss altogether ('I have seen it three times') and the duke went alone.

It happened, though, that at a reception for Canadian cultural notables the Queen got talking to Alice Munro and, learning that she was a novelist and short-story writer, requested one of her books, which she greatly enjoyed. Even better, it turned out there were many more where that came from and which Ms Munro readily supplied.

'Can there be any greater pleasure', she confided in her neighbour, the Canadian minister for overseas trade, 'than to come across an author one enjoys and then to find they have written not just one book or two, but at least a dozen?'

And all, though she did not say this, in paperback and so handbag size. A postcard was immediately dispatched to Norman telling him to get those few that were out of print from the library to await her return. Oh what treats!

But Norman was no longer there.

THE DAY before he was due to depart for the delights of Stockton-on-Tees Norman was called into Sir Kevin's office. The prime minister's special adviser had said that Norman should be sacked; Sir Kevin disliked the special adviser; he didn't like Norman much but he disliked the special adviser more, and it was this that saved Norman's bacon. Besides, Sir Kevin felt the sack was vulgar. Norman should not get the sack. There was a neater solution.

'Her Majesty is always anxious for the betterment of her employees,' the private secretary said benignly, 'and though she is more than satisfied with your work she wonders if you have ever thought of university?'

'University?' said Norman, who hadn't.

'Specifically, the University of East Anglia. They

have a very good English Department and indeed a School of Creative Writing. I have only to mention the names' – Sir Kevin looked down at his pad – 'of Ian McEwan, Rose Tremain and Kazuo Ishiguro . . .'

'Yes,' said Norman. 'We've read those.'

Wincing at the 'we', the private secretary said that he thought East Anglia would suit Norman very well.

'What with?' said Norman. 'I've no money.'

'That will not be a problem. Her Majesty, you see, is anxious not to hold you back.'

'I think I would rather stay here,' said Norman. 'It's an education in itself.'

'Ye-es,' said the private secretary. 'That will not be possible. Her Majesty has someone else in mind. Of course,' he smiled helpfully, 'your job in the kitchen is always open.'

Thus it was that when the Queen returned from Canada there was no Norman perched on his usual seat in the corridor. His chair was empty, not that there was a chair any more or that comforting pile of books she had got used to finding on her bedside table. More immediately, there was no one to whom she could discourse on the excellences of Alice Munro.

{ 69 }

'He wasn't popular, ma'am,' said Sir Kevin.

'He was popular with me,' said the Queen. 'Where has he gone?'

'No idea, ma'am.'

Norman, being a sensitive boy, wrote the Queen a long, chatty letter about the courses he was taking and the reading he had to do, but when he got a reply beginning 'Thank you for your letter in which Her Majesty was most interested' he knew he had been eased out, though whether by the Queen or her private secretary he wasn't sure.

If Norman didn't know who had engineered his departure, the Queen herself was in no doubt. Norman had gone the way of the travelling library and the case of books that ended up in Calgary. Like the book she had hidden behind the cushion in the state coach, he was lucky not to have been exploded. And she missed him, there was no doubt. But no letter came, no note, and there was nothing for it but grimly to go on. It wouldn't put a stop to her reading.

That the Queen was not more troubled by Norman's sudden departure might seem surprising and to reflect poorly on her character. But sudden absences and abrupt departures had always been a feature of her life. She was seldom told, for instance, when any-one was ill; distress and even fellow feeling something that being Queen entitled her to be without, or so her courtiers thought. When, as unfortunately happened, death did claim a servant or even sometimes a friend, it was often the first time that the Queen had heard that anything was amiss, 'We mustn't worry Her Majesty' a guiding principle for all her servants.

Norman of course had not died, just gone to the University of East Anglia, though, as the equerries saw it, this was much the same thing, as he had gone from Her Majesty's life and thus no longer existed, his name never mentioned by the Queen or anyone else. But the Queen should not be blamed on that score, on that the equerries agreed; the Queen should never be blamed. People died, people left and (more and more) people got into the papers. For her they were all departures of one sort or another. They left but she went on.

Less to her credit, before Norman's mysterious departure the Queen had begun to wonder if she was outgrowing him . . . or rather, out-reading him. Once upon a time he had been a humble and straightfor-ward guide to the world of books. He had advised her as to what to read and had not hesitated to say when he thought she was not ready for a book yet. Beckett, for instance, he had kept from her for a long while, and Nabokov, and it was only gradually he had introduced her to Philip Roth (with *Portnoy's Complaint* quite late on in the sequence).

More and more, though, she had read what she fancied and Norman had done the same. They talked about what they were reading but increasingly she felt her life and experience gave her the advantage; books could only take one so far. She had learned, too, that Norman's preferences could sometimes be suspect. Other things being equal he still tended to prefer gay authors, hence her acquaintance with Genet. Some she liked – the novels of Mary Renault, for instance, fascinated her – but others of a deviant persuasion she was less keen on: Denton Welch, for instance (a favourite of Norman's), whom she felt was rather unhealthy; Isherwood (no time for all the meditation). As a reader she was brisk and straightforward; she didn't want to *wallow* in anything.

With no Norman to talk to, the Queen now found she was conducting lengthier discussions with herself and putting more and more of her thoughts on paper, so that her notebooks multiplied and widened in scope. 'One recipe for happiness is to have no sense of entitlement.' To this she added a star and noted at the bottom of the page: 'This is not a lesson I have ever been in a position to learn.'

'I was giving the CH once, I think it was to Anthony Powell, and we were discussing bad behaviour. Notably well behaved himself and even conventional, he remarked that being a writer didn't excuse one from being a human being. Whereas (one didn't say this) being Queen does. I have to seem like a human being all the time, but I seldom have to be one. I have people to do that for me.'

In addition to thoughts such as these she found herself noting descriptions of people she met, not necessarily all of them famous: their oddities of behaviour, their turns of phrase, as well as the stories she was told, often in confidence. When some scandalous report about the royal family appeared in the newspapers the real facts went into her notebook. When some scandal escaped public notice, that too went down, and all of them told in that sensible, down-to-earth tone of voice she was coming to recognise and even relish as her own style.

In the absence of Norman her reading, though it did not falter, did change direction. While she still ordered books from the London Library and from booksellers, with Norman gone it was no longer their secret. Now she had to ask the lady-in-waiting, who spoke to the comptroller before drawing the petty cash. It was a wearisome process, which she would occasionally circumvent by asking one of the more peripheral grandchildren to get her books. They were happy to oblige and pleased to be taken notice of at all, the public scarcely knowing they existed. But more and more now the Queen began to take books out of her own libraries, particularly the one at Windsor, where, though the choice of modern books was not unlimited, the shelves were stacked with many editions of the classic texts, some of them, of course, autographed – Balzac, Turgenev, Fielding, Conrad, books which once she would have thought beyond her but which now she sailed through, pencil always in hand, and in the process, incidentally, becoming reconciled even to Henry James, whose divagations she now took in her stride: 'After all,' as she wrote in her notebook, 'novels are not necessarily written as the crow flies.' Seeing her sitting at the window to catch the last of the light, the librarian thought that a more assiduous reader these ancient shelves had not seen since the days of George III.

The librarian at Windsor had been one of many who had urged on Her Majesty the charms of Jane Austen, but being told on all sides how much ma'am would like her put ma'am off altogether. Besides she had handicaps as a reader of Jane Austen that were peculiarly her own. The essence of Jane Austen lies in minute social distinctions, distinctions which the Queen's unique position made it difficult for her to grasp. There was such a chasm between the monarch and even her grandest subject that the social differences beyond that were somewhat telescoped. So the social distinctions of which Jane Austen made so much seemed of even less consequence to the Queen than they did to the ordinary reader, thus making the novels much harder going. To begin with at any rate Jane Austen was practically a work of entomology, the characters not quite ants but seeming to the royal reader so much alike as to require a microscope. It was only as she gained in understanding both of literature and of human nature that they took on individuality and charm.

Feminism, too, got short shrift, at least to begin with and for the same reason, the separations of gender like the differences of class as nothing compared with the gulf that separated the Queen from the rest of humanity.

But whether it was Jane Austen or feminism or even Dostoevsky the Queen eventually got round to it and to much else besides, but never without regret. Years ago she had sat next to Lord David Cecil at a dinner in Oxford and had been at a loss for conversation. He, she found, had written books on Jane Austen and these days she would have relished the encounter. But Lord David was dead and so it was too late. Too late. It was all too late. But she went on, determined as ever and always trying to catch up.

THE HOUSEHOLD, too, went on, running as smoothly as it always did, the moves from London to Windsor to Norfolk to Scotland achieved with no seeming effort, at any rate on her part, so that sometimes she felt almost surplus to the procedure, the same transferences and translations accomplished regardless of the person at their centre. It was a ritual of departure and arrival in which she was just a piece of luggage; the most important piece, there was no disputing that, but luggage nevertheless.

In one respect these peregrinations went better than they had done in the past, in that the personage around whom they revolved generally had her nose in a book. She got into the car at Buckingham Palace and got out at Windsor without ever leaving the side of Captain Crouchback in the evacuation of Crete. She flew to Scotland happy in the (occasionally exasperating) company of Tristram Shandy, and when she got bored with him Trollope (Anthony) was never far away. It all made her a pliant and undemanding traveller. True, she wasn't always quite as on the dot as she used to be, and the motor waiting under the canopy in the courtyard was a familiar sight, the duke increasingly tetchy in the back. But when she eventually hurried into the car she was never tetchy; after all, she had her book.

Her household, though, had no such solace and the equerries in particular were becoming increasingly restive and critical. Urbane and exquisitely mannered though he is, the equerry is essentially only a stage manager; always aware when deference is due he (or occasionally she) knows, too, that this is a performance and he is in charge of it, with Her Majesty playing the leading role.

The audience or the spectators – and where the Queen is concerned everyone is a spectator – know that it is a performance, while liking to tell themselves that it isn't, quite, and to think, performance notwithstanding, that they have occasionally caught a glimpse of behaviour that is more 'natural', more 'real' – the odd overheard remark, for instance ('I could murder a gin and tonic,' from the late Queen Mother, 'Bloody dogs,' from the Duke of Edinburgh), or the Queen sitting down at a garden party and thankfully kicking off her shoes. In truth, of course, these supposedly unguarded moments are just as much a performance as the royal family at its most hieratic. This show, or sideshow, might be called playing at being normal and is as contrived as the most formal public appearance, even though those who witness or overhear it think that this is the Queen and her family at their most human and natural. Formal or informal, it is all part of that self-presentation in which the equerries collaborate and which, these apparently impromptu moments apart, is from the public's point of view virtually seamless.

It only gradually came home to the equerries that these supposedly sincere moments, glimpses of the Queen as she 'really is', were occurring less often. Diligently though Her Majesty might carry out all her duties, that was all she was doing, and never now pretending, as it were, to break ranks and seldom coming out with supposedly unrehearsed remarks ('Careful,' she might say as she pins a medal on a young man, 'I don't want to stab you through the heart'), remarks that could be taken home and cherished, along with the invitation card, the special car-park pass and the map of the palace precincts.

These days she was formal, smiling and seemingly sincere but without frills and with none of the supposedly off-the-cuff asides with which she was wont to enliven the proceedings. 'Poor show,' thought the equerries and that is exactly what they meant, 'a poor show' in which Her Majesty had turned in a dull performance. But they were not in a position to draw attention to this omission as they, too, colluded in the pretence that such moments were natural and unpremeditated, a genuine overflowing of Her Majesty's sense of fun.

It had been an investiture.

'Less spontaneous this morning, ma'am,' one of the bolder equerries ventured to say.

'Was I?' said the Queen, who would once have been most put out at even this mildest of criticisms, though these days it scarcely impinged. 'I think I know why it is. You see, Gerald, as they kneel one looks down on the tops of people's heads a good deal and from that perspective even the most unsympathetic personality seems touching: the beginnings of a bald patch, the hair growing over the collar. One's feelings are almost maternal.'

The equerry, with whom she'd never shared such confidences before and who ought to have been flattered, simply felt awkward and embarrassed. This was a truly human side to the monarch of which he'd never been previously aware and which (unlike its counterfeit versions) he did not altogether welcome. And whereas the Queen herself thought that such feelings probably arose out of her reading books, the young man felt it might be that she was beginning to show her age. Thus it was that the dawn of sensibility was mistaken for the onset of senility.

Immune to embarrassment herself, as she was to any that she might cause, the Queen would once not have noticed the young man's confusion. But observing it now she resolved in the future to share her thoughts less promiscuously, which was a pity in a way as it was what many in the nation longed for. Instead she determined to restrict her confidences to her notebooks, where they could do no harm.

The Queen had never been demonstrative; it was not in her upbringing; but more and more these days, particularly in the period following Princess Diana's death, she was being required to go public about feelings she would have preferred to keep to herself. At that time, though, she had not yet begun to read, and it was only now that she understood that her predicament was not unique and that she shared it, among others, with Cordelia. She wrote in her notebook: 'Though I do not always understand Shakespeare, Cordelia's "I cannot heave my heart into my mouth" is a sentiment I can readily endorse. Her predicament is mine.'

Though the Queen was always discreet about writing in her notebooks her equerry was not reassured. He had once or twice caught her at it and thought that this, too, pointed to potential derangement. What had Her Majesty to note down? She never used to do it and like any change of behaviour in the elderly it was readily put down to decay.

'Probably Alzheimer's,' said another of the young men. 'You have to write things down for them, don't you?' and this, taken together with Her Majesty's growing indifference to appearances, made her attendants fear the worst.

That the Queen might be thought to be suffering from Alzheimer's disease was shocking in the obvious way, the 'human' and compassionate way, but to Gerald and the other equerries it was more subtly deplorable. It seemed to him pitiable that Her Majesty, whose life had always been so sequestered, should now have to share this undignified depletion with so many of her subjects, her deterioration, he felt, deserving a royal enclosure where her behaviour (and that of monarchs generally) might be allowed a larger degree of latitude and even waywardness before it attracted the levelling denomination of

Alzheimer and his all-too-common disease. It could have been a syllogism, if Gerald had known what a syllogism was: Alzheimer's is common, the Queen is not common, therefore the Queen has not got Alzheimer's.

Nor had she, of course, and in fact her faculties had never been sharper and unlike her equerry she would certainly have known what a syllogism was.

Besides, apart from writing in her notebooks and her now fairly customary lateness, what did this deterioration amount to? A brooch repeated, say, or a pair of court shoes worn on successive days: the truth was Her Majesty didn't care, or didn't care as much, and herself not caring, her attendants, being human, began to care less, too, cutting corners as the Queen would never previously have countenanced. The Queen had always dressed with great care. She had an encyclopaedic knowledge of her wardrobe and her multiple accessories and was scrupulous in ringing the changes on her various outfits. No longer. An ordinary woman who wore the same frock twice in a fortnight would not be thought slipshod or negligent of appearances. But in the Queen, the permutations of whose wardrobe were worked out down to the last buckle, such repetitions signalled a dramatic falling away from her own self-imposed standards of decorum.

'Doesn't ma'am care?' said the maid boldly.

'Care about what?' said the Queen, which, while being an answer of sorts, did nothing to reassure the maid, convincing her that something was deeply amiss, so that like the equerries her personal attendants began to prepare for a lengthy decline.

STILL, THOUGH he saw her every week, the occasional want of variation in the Queen's attire and the sameness of her earrings went unnoticed by the prime minister.

It had not always been so, and at the start of his term of office he had frequently complimented the Queen on what Her Majesty was wearing and her always discreet jewellery. He was younger then, of course, and thought of it as flirting, though it was also a form of nerves. She was younger, too, but she was not nervous and had been long enough at the game to know that this was just a phase that most prime ministers went through (the exceptions being

Mr Heath and Mrs Thatcher) and that as the novelty of their weekly interviews diminished so, too, did the flirting.

It was another aspect of the myth of the Queen and her prime minister, the decline of the prime minister's attention to her personal appearance coinciding with his dwindling concern with what Her Majesty had to say, how the Queen looked and how the Queen thought, both of diminishing importance, so that, earrings or no earrings, making her occasional comments she felt not unlike an air hostess going through the safety procedures, the look on the prime minister's face that of benevolent and minimal attention from a passenger who has heard it all before.

The inattention, though, and the boredom were not all his, and as she had begun to read more, she resented the time these meetings took up and so thought to enliven the process by relating them to her studies and what she was learning about history.

This was not a good idea. The prime minister did not wholly believe in the past or in any lessons that might be drawn from it. One evening he was addressing her on the subject of the Middle East when she ventured to say, 'It is the cradle of civilisation, you know.'

'And shall be again, ma'am,' said the prime minister, 'provided we are allowed to persist,' and then bolted off down a side alley about the mileage of new sewage pipes that had been laid and the provision of electricity substations.

She interrupted again. 'One hopes this isn't to the detriment of the archaeological remains. Do you know about Ur?'

He didn't. So as he was going she found him a couple of books that might help. The following week she asked him if he had read them (which he hadn't).

'They were most interesting, ma'am.'

'Well, in that case we must find you some more. I find it fascinating.'

This time Iran came up and she asked him if he knew of the history of Persia, or Iran (he had scarcely even connected the two), and gave him a book on that besides, and generally began to take such an interest that after two or three sessions like this, Tuesday evenings, which he had hitherto looked forward to as a restful oasis in his week, now became fraught with apprehension. She even questioned him about the books as if they were homework. Finding he hadn't read them she smiled tolerantly.

'My experience of prime ministers, Prime Minister, is that, with Mr Macmillan the exception, they prefer to have their reading done for them.'

'One is busy, ma'am,' said the prime minister.

'One is busy,' she agreed and reached for her book. 'We will see you next week.'

Eventually Sir Kevin got a call from the special adviser.

'Your employer has been giving my employer a hard time.'

'Yes?'

'Yes. Lending him books to read. That's out of order.'

'Her Majesty likes reading.'

'I like having my dick sucked. I don't make the prime minister do it. Any thoughts, Kevin?'

'I will speak to Her Majesty.'

'You do that, Kev. And tell her to knock it off.'

Sir Kevin did not speak to Her Majesty, still less tell her to knock it off. Instead, swallowing his pride, he went to see Sir Claude.

IN THE little garden of his delightful seventeenth-century grace-and-favour cottage at Hampton Court Sir Claude Pollington was reading. Actually, he was meant to be reading, but he was dozing over a box of confidential documents sent over from the library at Windsor, a privilege accorded to him as an ancient royal servant, now ninety at least but still ostensibly working on his memoirs, tentatively entitled 'Drudgery Divine'.

Sir Claude had entered royal service straight from Harrow at the age of eighteen as a page to George V, one of his first tasks, as he was fond of recalling, being to lick the hinges with which that testy and punctilious monarch used to stick the stamps into his many albums. 'Were there a problem discovering my DNA,' he had once confided to Sue Lawley, 'one would only have to look behind the stamps in dozens of the royal albums, particularly, I recall, the stamps of Tanna Touva, which His Majesty thought vulgar and even common but which he nevertheless felt obliged to collect. Which was typical of His Majesty . . . conscientious to a fault.' He had then chosen a record of Master Ernest Lough singing 'O for the Wings of a Dove'.

In his little drawing room every surface sprouted framed photographs of the various royals whom Sir Claude had so loyally served. Here he was at Ascot, holding the King's binoculars; crouching in the heather as His Majesty drew a bead on a distant stag. This was him bringing up the rear as Queen Mary emerged from a Harrogate antique shop, the young Pollington's face hidden behind a parcel containing a Wedgwood vase, reluctantly bestowed on Her Majesty by the hapless dealer. Here he was, too, in a striped jersey, helping to crew the *Nahlin* on that fateful Mediterranean cruise, the lady in the yachting cap a Mrs Simpson – a photograph that tended to come and go, and which was never on view when, as often used to happen, Queen Elizabeth the Queen Mother dropped in for tea.

There was not much about the royal family to which Sir Claude had not been privy. After his service with George V he had been briefly in the household of Edward VIII and moved smoothly on into the service of his brother, George VI. He had done duty in many of the offices of the household, finally serving as private secretary to the Queen. Even when he had long retired his advice was frequently called on; he was a living embodiment of that establishment commendation, 'a safe pair of hands'.

Now, though, his hands shook rather and he was not as careful as he used to be about personal hygiene, and even sitting with him in the fragrant garden Sir Kevin had to catch his breath.

'Should we go inside?' said Sir Claude. 'There could be tea.'

'No, no,' said Sir Kevin hastily. 'Here is better.'

He explained the problem.

'Reading?' said Sir Claude. 'No harm in that, surely? Her Majesty takes after her namesake, the first Elizabeth. She was an avid reader. Of course, there were fewer books then. And Queen Elizabeth the Queen Mother, she liked a book. Queen Mary didn't, of course. Or George V. He was a great stamp collector. That's how I started, you know. Licking his hinges.'

Someone even older than Sir Claude brought out tea, which Sir Kevin prudently poured.

'Her Majesty is very fond of you, Sir Claude.'

'As I am of her,' said the old man. 'I have been in thrall to Her Majesty since she was a girl. All my life.'

And it had been a distinguished life, too, with a good war in which the young Pollington won several medals and commendations for bravery, serving finally on the general staff.

'I've served three queens,' he was fond of saying, 'and got on with them all. The only queen I could never get on with was Field Marshal Montgomery.'

'She listens to you,' said Sir Kevin, wondering if the sponge cake was reliable.

'I like to think so,' said Sir Claude. 'But what do I say? Reading. How curious. Tuck in.'

Just in time Sir Kevin realised that what he had taken for frosting was in fact mould and he managed to palm the cake into his briefcase.

'Perhaps you could remind her of her duty?'

'Her Majesty has never needed to be reminded of that. Too much duty if you ask me. Let me think . . .'

And the old man pondered while Sir Kevin waited.

It was some time before he realised that Sir Claude was asleep. He got up loudly.

'I will come,' said Sir Claude. 'It's a bit since I had an outing. You'll send a car?'

'Of course,' said Sir Kevin, shaking hands. 'Don't get up.'

As he went Sir Claude called after him.

'You're the New Zealand one, aren't you?'

'I GATHER', said the equerry, 'that it might be advisable if Your Majesty were to see Sir Claude in the garden.'

'In the garden?'

'Out of doors, ma'am. In the fresh air.'

The Queen looked at him. 'Do you mean he smells?'

'Apparently he does rather, ma'am.'

'Poor thing.' She wondered sometimes where they thought she'd been all her life. 'No. He must come up here.'

Though when the equerry offered to open a window she did not demur.

'What does he want to see me about?'

'I've no idea, ma'am.'

Sir Claude came in on his two sticks, bowing his head at the door and again when Her Majesty gave him her hand as she motioned him to sit down. Though her smile remained kindly and her manner unchanged, the equerry had not exaggerated.

'How are you, Sir Claude?'

'Very well, Your Majesty. And you, ma'am?'

'Very well.'

The Queen waited, but too much the courtier to introduce a subject unprompted Sir Claude waited too.

'What was it you wanted to see me about?'

While Sir Claude tried to remember, the Queen had time to notice the thin reef of dandruff that had gathered beneath his coat collar, the egg stains on his tie and the drift of scurf that lay in his large pendulous ear. Whereas once upon a time such frailties would have been beneath her notice and gone unremarked now they obtruded on her gaze, ruffling her composure and even causing her distress. Poor man. And he had fought at Tobruk. She must write it down.

'Reading, ma'am.'

'I beg your pardon.'

'Your Majesty has started reading.'

'No, Sir Claude. One has always read. Only these days one is reading more.'

Now, of course, she knew why he had come and who had put him up to it, and from being an object wholly of pity this witness to half her life now took his place among her persecutors; all compassion fled and she recovered her composure.

'I see no harm in reading in itself, ma'am.'

'One is relieved to hear it.'

'It's when it's carried to extremes. There's the mischief.'

'Are you suggesting one rations one's reading?'

'Your Majesty has led such an exemplary life. That it should be reading that has taken Your Majesty's fancy is almost by the way. Had you invested any pursuit with similar fervour eyebrows must have been raised.'

'They might. But then one has spent one's life not raising eyebrows. One feels sometimes that that is not much of a boast.'

'Ma'am has always liked racing.'

'True. Only one's rather gone off it at the moment.'

'Oh,' said Sir Claude. 'That's a shame.' Then, seeing a possible accommodation between racing and reading, 'Her Majesty the Queen Mother used to be a big fan of Dick Francis.'

'Yes,' said the Queen. 'I've read one or two, though they only take one so far. Swift, I discover, is very good about horses.'

Sir Claude nodded gravely, not having read Swift and reflecting that he seemed to be getting nowhere.

They sat for a moment in silence, but it was long enough for Sir Claude to fall asleep. This had seldom happened to the Queen and when it had (a government minister nodding off alongside her at some ceremony, for instance) her reaction had been brisk and unsympathetic. She was often tempted to fall asleep, as with her job who wouldn't be, but now, rather than wake the old man she just waited, listening to his laboured breathing and wondering how long it would be before infirmity overtook her and she became similarly incapable. Sir Claude had come with a message, she understood that and resented it, but perhaps he was a message in his own person, a portent of the unpalatable future.

She picked up her notebook from the desk and dropped it on the floor. Sir Claude woke up nodding and smiling as if appreciating something the Queen had just said.

'How are your memoirs?' said the Queen. Sir Claude's memoirs had been on the go for so long they had become a joke in the household. 'How far have you got?'

'Oh, they're not consecutive, ma'am. One does a little every day.'

He didn't, of course, and it was really only to forestall yet another probing royal question that he now said what he did. 'Has Your Majesty ever considered writing?'

'No,' said the Queen, though this was a lie. 'Where would one find the time?'

'Ma'am has found time for reading.'

This was a rebuke and the Queen did not take kindly to rebukes, but for the moment she overlooked it.

'What should one write?'

'Your Majesty has had an interesting life.'

'Yes,' said the Queen. 'One has.'

The truth was Sir Claude had no notion of what the Queen should write or whether she should write at all, and he had only suggested writing in order to get her off reading and because in his experience writing seldom got done. It was a cul-de-sac. He had been writing his memoirs for twenty years and hadn't even written fifty pages.

'Yes,' he said firmly. 'Ma'am must write. But can I give Your Majesty a tip? Don't start at the beginning.

That's the mistake I made. Start off in the middle. Chronology is a great deterrent.'

'Was there anything else, Sir Claude?'

The Queen gave her wide smile. The interview was over. How the Queen conveyed this information had always been a mystery to Sir Claude, but it was as plain as if a bell had rung. He struggled to his feet as the equerry opened the door, bowed his head, then when he reached the door turned and bowed his head again, then slowly stumped down the corridor on his two sticks, one of them a present from the Queen Mother.

Back in the room the Queen opened the window wider and let the breeze blow in from the garden. The equerry returned, and raising her eyebrows the Queen indicated the chair on which Sir Claude had been sitting, now with a damp patch staining the satin. Silently the young man bore the chair away, while the Queen gathered up her book and her cardigan preparatory to going into the garden.

By the time the equerry returned with another chair she had stepped out onto the terrace. He put it down and with the skill of long practice quickly set the room to rights, spotting as he did so the Queen's notebook lying on the floor. He picked it up and before replacing it on the desk stood for a moment wondering in the Queen's absence if he might take a peep at the contents. Except at that moment Her Majesty reappeared in the doorway.

'Thank you, Gerald,' she said and held out her hand.

He gave her the book and she went out.

'Shit,' said Gerald. 'Shit. Shit. Shit.'

This note of self-reproach was not inappropriate as within days Gerald was no longer in attendance on Her Majesty and indeed no longer in the household at all, but back with his scarcely remembered regiment yomping in the rain over the moors of Northumberland. The speed and ruthlessness of his almost Tudor dispatch sent, as Sir Kevin would have put it, the right message and at least put paid to any further rumours of senile decay. Her Majesty was herself again.

NOTHING Sir Claude had said carried any weight, but still she found herself thinking about it that evening at the Royal Albert Hall, where there was a special promenade concert in her honour. In the past music had never been much of a solace and had always been tinged with obligation, the repertoire familiar largely from concerts like this she had had to attend. Tonight, though, the music seemed more relevant.

This was a voice, she thought, as a boy played the clarinet: Mozart, a voice everybody in the hall knew and recognised though Mozart had been dead two hundred years. And she remembered Helen Schlegel in *Howards End* putting pictures to Beethoven at the concert in the Queen's Hall that Forster describes, Beethoven's another voice that everyone knew.

The boy finished, the audience applauded and, clapping too, she leaned over towards another of the party as if sharing her appreciation. But what she wanted to say was that, old as she was, renowned as she was, no one knew her voice. And in the car taking them back she suddenly said: 'I have no voice.'

'Not surprised,' said the duke. 'Too damned hot. Throat, is it?'

It was a sultry night and unusually for her she woke in the early hours unable to sleep.

The policeman in the garden, seeing the light go on, turned on his mobile as a precaution.

She had been reading about the Brontës and what a hard time they had had of it when they were children, but she didn't feel that would send her off to sleep again and, looking for something else, saw in the corner of the bookshelf the book by Ivy Compton-Burnett which she had borrowed from the travelling library and which Mr Hutchings had given her all that time ago. It had been hard going and had nearly sent her to sleep then, she remembered, so perhaps it would do the trick again.

Far from it, and the novel she had once found slow now seemed refreshingly brisk, dry still but astringently so, with Dame Ivy's no-nonsense tone reassuringly close to her own. And it occurred to her (as next day she wrote down) that reading was, among other things, a muscle and one that she had seemingly developed. She could read the novel with ease and great pleasure, laughing at remarks (they were hardly jokes) that she had not even noticed before. And through it all she could hear the voice of Ivy Compton-Burnett, unsentimental, severe and wise. She could hear her voice as clearly as earlier in the evening she had heard the voice of Mozart. She closed the book. And once again she said out loud: 'I have no voice.'

And somewhere in West London where these things are recorded a transcribing and expressionless typist thought it was an odd remark and said as if in reply: 'Well, if you don't, dear, I don't know who does.'

Back in Buckingham Palace the Queen waited a moment or two, then switched off the light, and under the catalpa tree in the grounds the policeman saw the light go out and turned off his mobile.

In the darkness it came to the Queen that, dead, she would exist only in the memories of people. She who had never been subject to anyone would now be on a par with everybody else. Reading could not change that – though writing might.

Had she been asked if reading had enriched her life she would have had to say yes, undoubtedly, though adding with equal certainty that it had at the same time drained her life of all purpose. Once she had been a self-assured single-minded woman knowing where her duty lay and intent on doing it for as long as she was able. Now all too often she was in two minds. Reading was not doing, that had always been the trouble. And old though she was she was still a doer.

She switched the light on again and reached for her notebook and wrote: 'You don't put your life into your books. You find it there.'

Then she went to sleep.

IN THE WEEKS that followed it was noticeable that the Queen was reading less, if at all. She was pensive and abstracted even, but not because her mind was on what she was reading. She no longer carried a book with her wherever she went and the piles of volumes that had accumulated on her desk were shelved, sent back to the libraries or otherwise dispersed.

But, reading or not, she still spent long hours at her desk, sometimes looking at her notebooks and occasionally writing in them, though she knew, without quite spelling it out to herself, that her writing would be even less popular than her reading, and did anyone knock at the door she immediately swept them into her desk drawer before saying, 'Come in.'

She found, though, that when she had written something down, even if it was just an entry in her notebook, she was happy as once she would have been happy after doing some reading. And it came to her again that she did not want simply to be a reader. A reader was next door to being a spectator whereas when she was writing she was doing, and doing was her duty.

Meanwhile she was often in the library, particularly at Windsor, looking through her old desk diaries, the albums of her innumerable visits, her archive in fact.

'Is there anything specific that Your Majesty is looking for?' said the librarian after he had brought her yet another pile of material.

'No,' said the Queen. 'One is just trying to remember what it was like. Though what "it" is one isn't sure either.'

'Well, if Your Majesty does remember, then I hope you will tell me. Or better still, ma'am, write it down. Your Majesty is a living archive.'

Though she felt he could have expressed this more tactfully, she knew what he meant and reflected, too, that here was someone else who was urging her to write. It was almost becoming a duty, and she had always been very good at duty, until, that is, she started to read. Still, to be urged to write and to be urged to publish are two different things and nobody so far was urging her to do the latter.

Seeing the books disappear from her desk and having once more something approaching Her Majesty's whole attention were welcome to Sir Kevin and indeed to the household in general. Timekeeping did not improve, it's true, and the Queen's wardrobe still tended to be a little wayward ('I'd outlaw that cardigan,' said her maid). But Sir Kevin shared in the general impression that for all these persistent shortcomings Her Majesty had seen off her infatuation with books and had returned to normal.

She stayed that autumn for a few days at Sandringham, as she was scheduled to make a royal visit to the city of Norwich. There was a service in the cathedral, a walkabout in the pedestrian precinct and before she had luncheon at the university she opened a new fire station.

Seated between the vice-chancellor and the professor of creative writing she was mildly surprised when over her shoulder came a bony wrist and red hand that were very familiar, proffering a prawn cocktail.

'Hello, Norman,' she said.

'Your Majesty,' said Norman correctly, and smoothly presented the lord lieutenant with his prawn cocktail, before going on down the table.

'Your Majesty knows Seakins then, ma'am?' said the professor of creative writing.

'One did,' said the Queen, saddened a little that Norman seemed to have made no progress in the world at all and was seemingly back in a kitchen, even if it was not hers.

'We thought', said the vice-chancellor, 'that it would be rather a treat for the students if they were to serve the meal. They will be paid, of course, and it's all experience.'

'Seakins', said the professor, 'is very promising. He has just graduated and is one of our success stories.'

The Queen was a little put out that, despite her bright smile, serving the bœuf en croûte Norman seemed determined not to catch her eye, and the same went for the poire belle-Hélène. And it came to her that for some reason Norman was sulking, behaviour she had seldom come across except in children and the occasional cabinet minister. Subjects seldom sulked to the Queen as they were not entitled to, and once upon a time it would have taken them to the Tower.

A few years ago she would never have noticed what Norman was doing or anybody else either, and if she took note of it now it was because she knew more of people's feelings than she used to and could put herself in someone else's place. Though it still didn't explain why he was so put out.

'Books are wonderful, aren't they?' she said to the vice-chancellor, who concurred.

'At the risk of sounding like a piece of steak,' she said, 'they tenderise one.'

He concurred again, though with no notion of what she was on about.

'I wonder', she turned to her other neighbour, 'whether as professor of creative writing you would agree that if reading softens one up, writing does the reverse. To write you have to be tough, do you not?' Surprised to find himself discussing his own subject, the professor was momentarily at a loss. The Queen waited. 'Tell me,' she wanted to say, 'tell me I am right.' But the lord lieutenant was rising to wait upon her and the room shuffled to its feet. No one was going to tell her, she thought. Writing, like reading, was something she was going to have to do on her own.

Though not quite, and afterwards Norman is sent for, and the Queen, her lateness now proverbial but catered for in the schedule, spends half an hour being updated on his university career, including the circumstances that brought him to East Anglia in the first place. It is arranged that he will come to Sandringham the following day, where the Queen feels that now he has begun to write he may be in a position to assist her once again.

Between one day and the next, though, she sacked somebody else, and Sir Kevin came into his office in the morning to find his desk cleared. Though Norman's stint at the university had been advantageous Her Majesty did not like being deceived, and though the real culprit was the prime minister's special adviser Sir Kevin carried the can. Once it would have brought him to the block; these days it brought him a ticket back to New Zealand and an appointment as high commissioner. It was the block but it took longer.

SLIGHTLY TO her own surprise that year the Queen turned eighty. It was not a birthday that went unmarked and various celebrations were organised, some more to Her Majesty's liking than others, with her advisers tending to regard the birthday as just another opportunity to ingratiate the monarchy with the always fickle public.

It was not surprising, then, that the Queen decided to throw a party of her own and to assemble all those who had had the privilege of advising her over the years. This was in effect a party for the Privy Council, appointment to which is for life, thus making it a large and unwieldy body that in its entirety meets seldom and then only on occasions of some gravity. But there was nothing, thought the Queen, that would preclude her having them all to tea, and a serious tea at that, ham, tongue, mustard and cress, scones, cakes and even trifle. Much preferable to dinner, she thought, and cosier altogether.

Nobody was told to dress up, though Her Majesty was as groomed and immaculate as she had been in the old days. But what a lot of advice she had had over the years, she thought, as she surveyed the crowded assembly; there were so many who had tendered it that they could only be accommodated in one of the grandest rooms in the palace, with the sumptuous tea laid out in two adjoining salons. She moved happily among her guests, unsupported by any other member of the royal family, who, though many of them were privy councillors, had not been invited. 'I see quite enough of them as it is,' she said, 'whereas I never see all of you and, short of my dying, there's no occasion when you're all likely to see each other. Do try the trifle. It's wicked.' Seldom had she been in such good spirits.

The prospect of a proper tea had fetched the privy councillors out in greater numbers than had been anticipated: dinner would have been a chore, whereas tea was a treat. There was such a crowd that chairs were in short supply, and there was a lot of running to and fro by the staff in order to get everybody seated, though this turned out to be part of the fun. Some sat on the usual gilt party chairs, but others found themselves ensconced on a priceless Louis XV bergère or a monogrammed hall chair brought in from the vestibule, with one former lord chancellor ending up perched on a little cork-topped stool brought down from a bathroom.

The Queen placidly surveyed all these goings-on, not quite on a throne but certainly on a chair larger than anyone else's. She had brought her tea in with her and sipped and chatted until at last everyone had made themselves comfortable.

'I know that I've been well advised over the years but I hadn't realised quite how numerously. What a crowd!'

'Perhaps, ma'am, we should all sing "Happy Birthday"!' said the prime minister, who was naturally sitting in the front row.

'Don't let's get carried away,' said Her Majesty. 'Though it is true one is eighty and this is a sort of birthday party. But quite what there is to celebrate I'm not sure. I suppose one of the few things to be said for it is that one has at least achieved an age at which one can die without people being shocked.'

There was polite laughter at this and the Queen herself smiled. 'I think', she said, 'that more shouts of "No, No" might be appropriate.'

So somebody obliged and there was more complacent laughter as the nation's most distinguished tasted the joys of being teased by the nation's most eminent.

'One has had, as you all know, a long reign. In fifty years and more I have gone through, I do not say seen off' – (laughter) – 'ten prime ministers, six arch-bishops of Canterbury, eight speakers and, though you may not consider this a comparable statistic, fifty-three corgis – a life, as Lady Bracknell says, crowded with incident.'

The audience smiled comfortably, chuckling now and again. This was a bit like school, primary school anyway.

'And of course,' said the Queen, 'it goes on, not a week passing without something of interest, a scan-dal, a cover-up or even a war. And since this is one's birthday you must not even think of looking peeved' – (the prime minister was studying the ceiling and the home secretary the carpet) – 'for one has a long perspective and it was ever thus. At eighty things do not occur; they recur.

'However, as some of you may know, I have always disliked waste. One not wholly mythical version of my character has me going round Buckingham Palace switching off the lights, the implication being that one is mean, though these days it could better be put down to an awareness of global warming. But disliking waste as I do puts me in mind of all the experiences I have had, many of them unique to me, the fruit of a lifetime in which one has been, if only as a spectator, very close to events. Most of that experience' – and Her Majesty tapped her immaculately coiffed head – 'most of it is up here. And one wouldn't want it to go to waste. So the question is, what happens to it?'

The prime minister opened his mouth as if to speak and indeed half rose from his chair.

'The question', said the Queen, 'was rhetorical.'

He sank back.

'As some of you may know, over the last few years I have become an avid reader. Books have enriched my life in a way that one could never have expected. But books can only take one so far and now I think it is time that from being a reader I become, or try to become, a writer.'

The prime minister was bobbing again and the Queen, reflecting that this was what generally happened to her with prime ministers, graciously yielded the floor.

'A book, Your Majesty. Oh yes, yes. Reminiscences

of your childhood, ma'am, and the war, the bombing of the palace, your time in the WAAF.'

'The ATS,' corrected the Queen.

'The armed forces, whatever,' the prime minister galloped on. 'Then your marriage, the dramatic circumstances in which you learned you were Queen. It will be sensational. And', he chortled, 'there's not much doubt that it will be a bestseller.'

'*The* bestseller,' trumped the home secretary. 'All over the world.'

'Ye-es,' said the Queen, 'only' – and she relished the moment – 'that isn't quite the kind of book one had in mind. That is a book, after all, that anyone can write and several people have – all of them, to my mind, tedious in the extreme. No, I was envisaging a book of a different sort.'

The prime minister, unsquashed, raised his eyebrows in polite interest. Maybe the old girl meant a travel book. They always sold well.

The Queen settled herself down. 'I was thinking of something more radical. More . . . challenging.'

'Radical' and 'challenging' both being words that often tripped off the prime minister's tongue, he still felt no alarm.

'Have any of you read Proust?' asked the Queen of the room.

Somebody deaf whispered 'Who?' and a few hands went up, the prime minister's not among them, and seeing this, one young member of the cabinet who had read Proust and was about to put his hand up didn't, because he thought it would do him no good at all to say so.

The Queen counted. 'Eight, nine – ten' – most of them, she noted, relics of much older cabinets. 'Well, that's something, though I'm hardly surprised. Had I asked Mr Macmillan's cabinet that question I'm sure a dozen hands would have gone up, including his. However that's hardly fair, as I hadn't read Proust at that time either.'

'I've read Trollope,' said a former foreign secretary.

'One is glad to hear it,' said the Queen, 'but Trollope is not Proust.' The home secretary, who had read neither, nodded sagely.

'Proust's is a long book, though, water-skiing permitting, you could get through it in the summer recess. At the end of the novel Marcel, who narrates it, looks back on a life that hasn't really amounted to much and resolves to redeem it by writing the novel which we have just in fact read, in the process unlocking some of the secrets of memory and remembrance.

'Now one's life, though one says it oneself, has, unlike Marcel's, amounted to a great deal, but like him I feel nevertheless that it needs redeeming by analysis and reflection.'

'Analysis?' said the prime minister.

'And reflection,' said the Queen.

Having thought of a joke that he knew would go down well in the House of Commons, the home secretary ventured on it here. 'Are we to assume that Your Majesty has decided to write this account because of something you read in a book, and a French book at that? Haw haw.'

There were one or two answering sniggers, but the Queen did not appear to notice that a joke had actually been made (as indeed it scarcely had). 'No, Home Secretary. But then books, as I'm sure you know, seldom prompt a course of action. Books generally just confirm you in what you have, perhaps unwittingly, decided to do already. You go to a book to have your convictions corroborated. A book, as it were, closes the book.'

Some of the councillors, long since out of government, were thinking that this was not the woman they remembered serving and were fascinated accordingly. But for the most part the gathering sat in uneasy silence, few of them having any idea what she was talking about. And the Queen knew it. 'You're puzzled,' she said, unperturbed, 'but I promise you, you do know this in your own sphere.'

Once again they were in school and she was their teacher. 'To inquire into the evidence for something on which you have already decided is the unacknowledged premise of every public inquiry, surely?'

The youngest minister laughed, then wished he hadn't. The prime minister wasn't laughing. If this was to be the tone of what the Queen was planning to write there was no telling what she was going to say. 'I still think you would do better just to tell your story, ma'am,' he said weakly.

'No,' said the Queen. 'I am not interested in facile reminiscence. It will, I hope, be something more thoughtful. Though when I say thoughtful I don't mean considerate. Joke.'

Nobody laughed and the smile on the prime minister's face had become a ghastly grin.

'Who knows,' said the Queen cheerfully, 'it might stray into literature.'

'I would have thought', said the prime minister, 'that Your Majesty was above literature.'

'Above literature?' said the Queen. 'Who is above literature? You might as well say one was above humanity. But, as I say, my purpose is not primarily literary: analysis and reflection. What about those ten prime ministers?' She smiled brightly. 'There is much to reflect on there. One has seen the country go to war more times than I like to recall. That, too, bears thinking about.'

Still she smiled, though if anyone followed suit, it was the oldest ones who had the least to worry about.

'One has met and indeed entertained many visiting heads of state, some of them unspeakable crooks and blackguards and their wives not much better.' This at least raised some rueful nods.

'One has given one's white-gloved hand to hands that were steeped in blood and conversed politely with men who have personally slaughtered children. One has waded through excrement and gore; to be Queen, I have often thought the one essential item of equipment a pair of thigh-length boots.

'One is often said to have a fund of common sense but that's another way of saying that one doesn't have much else and accordingly, perhaps, I have at the instance of my various governments been forced to participate if only passively in decisions I consider ill-advised and often shameful. Sometimes one has felt like a scented candle, sent in to perfume a regime, or aerate a policy, monarchy these days just a government-issue deodorant.

'I am the Queen and head of the Commonwealth, but there have been many times in the last fifty years when that has made me feel not pride but shame. However' – and here she stood up – 'we must not lose our sense of priorities and this is a party after all, so before I continue shall we now have some champagne?'

The champagne was superb but, seeing that one of the pages doing the serving was Norman, the prime minister lost all taste for it and slipped along the corridor to the toilet, where he got on his mobile to the attorney general. The lawyer did much to reassure him, and fortified by his legal advice the prime minister was able to pass the message round the members of the cabinet, so that when in due course Her Majesty came back into the room it was a more resilient group that awaited her.

'We've been talking about what you said, ma'am,' began the prime minister.

'All in good time,' said the Queen. 'One hasn't quite finished. I wouldn't want you to think that what I am planning to write and indeed have already started writing is some cheap, tell-tale life-in-the-palace nonsense beloved of the tabloids. No. One has never written a book before but one hopes that it will' – she paused – 'transcend its circumstances and stand on its own, a tangential history of its times and, you'll perhaps be reassured to learn, far from exclusively to do with politics or the events of one's life. I'd like to talk about books, too, and people. But not gossip. I don't care for gossip. A roundabout book. I think it was E. M. Forster who said: "Tell all the truth but tell it slant, success in circuit lies." Or was it', she asked the room, 'Emily Dickinson?'

Unsurprisingly, the room did not answer.

'But one mustn't talk about it or it will never get written.'

It was no comfort to the prime minister to reflect that whereas most people when claiming to want to write a book would never get it written, with the Queen and her terrible sense of duty it could be guaranteed that she would.

'Now, Prime Minister,' she turned to him gaily, 'you were saying?'

The prime minister rose. 'Respectful as we are of your intentions, ma'am' – the prime minister's tone was casual and friendly – 'I think I have to remind you that you are in a unique position.'

'I seldom forget it,' said the Queen. 'Go on.'

'The monarch has, I think I'm right in saying, never published a book.'

The Queen shook her finger at him, a gesture she remembered in the moment of making it that was a mannerism of Noël Coward's. 'That isn't quite true, Prime Minister. My ancestor Henry VIII, for instance, wrote a book. Against heresy. That is why one is still called Defender of the Faith. So, too, did my namesake Elizabeth I.'

The prime minister was about to protest.

'No, one knows it isn't the same, but my great-grandmother Queen Victoria, she wrote a book also, *Leaves from a Highland Journal*, and a pretty tedious book it is, too, and so utterly without offence as to be almost unreadable. It's not a model one would want to follow. And then of course' – and the Queen looked hard at her first minister – 'there was my uncle the Duke of Windsor. He wrote a book, *A King's Story*, the history of his marriage and subsequent adventures. If nothing else, that surely counts as a precedent?'

Furnished with the advice of the attorney general on this very point, the prime minister smiled and almost apologetically made his objection. 'Yes, ma'am, I agree, but the difference, surely, is that His Royal Highness wrote the book as Duke of Windsor. He could only write it because he had abdicated.'

'Oh, did I not say that?' said the Queen. 'But . . . why do you think you're all here?'